LAKE OF STONE

BOOK III
OF
SEEKING THE JEWEL FISH

K. EASTKOTT

Seeking the Jewel Fish

LAKE OF STONE

BOOK III
OF
SEEKING THE JEWEL FISH

K. EASTKOTT

ESCAPADE PRESS

(AN IMPRINT OF)

POBLESECBOOKS

Published by Escapade Press, an imprint of Poble Sec Books, in 2016. First published as an e-book in 2015.

British Library Cataloguing in Publication Data

A CIP catalogue record for this book is available from the British Library.

www.poblesecbooks.com

ISBNs:
978-0-9576551-9-5 (IS print);
978-0-9576551-6-4 (KDP print);
978-0-9576551-5-7 (.epub).

FOR BRIANNA

I.

COMPROMISING CONVERSATIONS

As Patrick drove over the freeway bridge at seven-fifty that morning, he saw what looked like a fluffy, dirty-gray carpet winding along the Mauri River valley. It was smoke, rolling thick and heavy across the landscape. Turning off, he eased his battered station wagon into the factory parking lot, between fire engines, police cars, and an ambulance. The scene was no less than he had been led to expect from the police call to his home twenty minutes earlier.

The ambulance's rear door was open, and a blackened figure wrapped in blankets was sitting just inside. As he approached, the young woman looked his way with a mixture of hostility, bravado, and dread.

"Hello. It's Rena, isn't it?" he asked with a smile.

"That's right, but I'm not going to talk to you, mister. Not till I see you and your wife's brat in court."

"The situation is terrible, isn't it? But I mainly came down here because I just wanted to check that you were all right. How are you feeling?"

He actually had little idea of what the situation truly

was. The first he had known that his stepdaughter was missing was when the police had called and told him she was a suspected arsonist. So he kept silent now, simply raising his eyebrows at Rena, hoping she would spill some much-needed information.

She looked at him suspiciously, but finally answered.

"Well, you should ask, mister.... And no, I'm not all right, since you're asking. But you guys will be worse off. You should be shaking cos' of the trouble your daughter's in. You see that?" She swept an arm toward the burning laboratory. "A progressive, economic miracle destroyed by a couple of kids. A source of employment for the whole area ... a project that was taking our country forward by leaps and bounds ... and a pair of brats get in there, and millions of millions of bucks ... KA-BOOMBA ... up in smoke!"

"But aren't you security? Wasn't it your job to keep potential troublemakers off the premises?"

"What are you saying? They sneaked in.... It wasn't my fault! Don't try and blame it on me, mister. You should bring up your kids better.... They're a danger to society!"

Patrick realized this was going the wrong way. He wanted to calm her down.

"I don't suppose you know—"

"Where your kids are? That proves my point exactly. You've lost them, haven't you?"

"I know where my stepson is!" Patrick snapped. "In hospital, in a very delicate state! I'm asking you about Jade because you are the last person to have seen her since..."—he waved his arm at the fire—"that."

"Can't help you, mister."

Patrick wanted to scream at the belligerent girl, but he knew it wouldn't make a shred of difference to her attitude. If she had any inkling where Jade was, she was not about to let on. He huffed in desperation, but then, gazing out across the field, saw another avenue of investigation, one that might offer him better results.

"Thank you, Rena, for your time. I hope you're better soon. You can be sure I'll talk to Jade when I find her."

"You do that, mister. Cos she's a menace, a menace to society! And I want compensation!"

Patrick meandered around the site. Firefighters still had their hoses directed on the blaze. No more flames were visible, but smoke continued to pour from the rubble. The entire building had collapsed in on itself, except for the two tall chimneys—now blackened — that emerged from the billowing smoke. Patrick couldn't get close to the river because of the smoke, but he eased his way around the police cordon and stepped out across the paddocks. A couple of figures were sitting in the grass about ten yards away with their backs to him.

"... Gees, Head! It's simple. Just listen to me and repeat it: We were out fishing, right? Early morning ..."

"Why this morning? We wouldn't of got paid by Dr. Hagues if we'd of gone fishing."

"Alibi, Head.... It's an alibi! Okay ... so we're out fishing, and we see these two come running out of the laboratory and jump into a speedboat they've got tied up there ..."

"Where?"

"On the bank, of course. They aren't going to tie it up in the middle of the river, are they, where they'd have to swim to it!"

"No, where are we fishing?"

"Who cares?"

"Well, we might not be able to see them from where we are."

"Good point, good point ..."

"And what about that canoe?"

"I told you, there's no canoe!"

"Then how do they get away?"

"In a speedboat, remember? A speedboat!"

"What speedboat?"

"The one I just invent—"

"Hi, boys!"

They spun on their backsides, shocked to be caught in the midst of such bare-handed fabrication.

"Uh, hello, Mr. ..." the Head started to say.

"S'okay, Head. I'll take it from here. What do you want?"

"I just wanted to check you boys weren't hurt at all by this terrible accident."

Screwdriver's eyes narrowed.

No.... What's it to you?"

"Well, as a resident of the bay, I feel concerned ..."

"Yeah, right. More like you're hoping we're not gonna lay charges against the kid. That it?"

"I just overheard what you were saying, that there was another reason you were really on the river?"

Screwdriver just squinted at Patrick.

"Suppose, Mr. Malone, you just tell us ... or the police, where Jade is ... and that vandal friend of hers."

"You don't need to worry about that. That's between us and the police."

"Yeah, right. Your girl's done a runner.... You don't know."

"That's none of your business!"

This wasn't how he'd hoped the conversation would go. Screwdriver seemed more intelligent than Patrick had bargained for. But he knew they must have some clue as to where Jade had gone to ground. So he tried again:

"So did you recognize their boat? A speedboat, you said?"

"Yeah," Screwdriver snorted. He seemed prepared to play Patrick's game. "Yeah, a flash model, millionaire style, you know?"

Patrick looked glum.

"They could have gone anywhere in that."

"Yep. Even down. It was a light boat, and they drove bang smack into the center of that storm that was hanging around out there this morning. Sorry, I can't help you out anymore, Mr. Malone," he smirked.

"That's okay, boys. Thanks for the information."

Patrick was pleased to note that Screwdriver looked suddenly worried, wondering whether he had let any important fact slip. Patrick had probably lost that battle. He didn't feel he had learned anything, but he got a malicious pleasure from keeping the snide-mouthed youth on the back foot. At least now he knew that they were covering up something, probably something illegal. Jade would not be involved with that, but she might have wanted to expose Rena and her crew. There was a good chance that was the reason she had sneaked out of the house and got into this mess. She and her friends Darren and Miguel were not at all on friendly terms with the older gang.

He left them and began walking down toward the river mouth, in the direction of Pine Bluff. His cell phone rang.

"Hello? Patrick?"

"Hi, love, … How's Kyle?"

There was a pause.

"He's still in the coma. They've been talking about various options … things they could try, but ... well, no change yet. Any news of Jade?"

"I've been talking to the security guard and her mates. Sorry, but nothing to report. I'm going to have a bit more of a scout around the coast. I'll try and hunt out one of her running buddies, Darren, or Miguel, see if they can help."

"Okay, call me if you learn anything. Love you."

"Will do. Love you too."

Patrick rang off and tried to recall exactly where in Mauri Cove Jade's two best mates lived.

2.
THE SEARCH

Unbreakfasted, Miguel sat in a tiny dinghy braving a choppy sea a mile offshore, and wondered how the day had conspired to place him here.

His arm, trapped in a plaster cast, was killing him. He'd tried sticking meat skewers down into it to alleviate the itching, but nothing worked for long. Four weeks ago, Rena, that sadistic security guard down at Synengine Energies had condemned him to a life of not being able to ride his bike, cut his own food, or even dress himself properly—plus this perpetual itching. He was bored with TV and had beaten every last game on his console. For all of this, for putting his arm in a cast, he owed her. Big time. But she was also part of the reason he was here.

Back in the days when he, Jade, and Darren used to play on the construction site of the laboratory that was happily burning today, it had seemed like a fun game. None of them had realized, as they dodged up and down the concrete channels and earthworks on the building site, that they were making such a vengeful enemy of Rena. Any sort of an enemy is bad news in a place as tiny as Mauri Cove, but you'd have to drive a long way to come across anyone with a reputation as mean as hers.

When he got up that morning, it had been all over the TV. As the camera panned across the beach where they normally went to surf, the headlines had seemed surreal:

ARSON ATTACK ON MAURI COVE RESEARCH
FACILITY: TWO MISSING, ONE HOSPITALIZED

The commentator's voice had that note of concerned urgency that tried to convince listeners that the very fabric of our civilization was crumbling before our eyes:

"In the early hours of this morning, a vindictive arson attack took place on the new experimental research facility that was recently inaugurated at Mauri Cove. The research center, which had been working on a prototype for a groundbreaking synthetic fuel that would produce no carbon emissions, was torched at approximately seven a.m. One security guard on the site needed to be attended for minor burns while police are investigating several leads, as well as the disappearance of a female youth who's a resident of Mauri Cove and an unidentified male. Anybody who has information as to their whereabouts is asked to contact the police immediately."

He had been on his way to pour his cornflakes when a knocking on the door interrupted him. Since his father was away on business and his mom had left for work two hours earlier, it was Miguel who opened the door to two police officers.

"Can we come in?" the burly one asked, barging past him in a way that Miguel was sure wouldn't have happened to an adult. Miguel recognized him: It was Officer Schreub, who had hauled Jade and Darren and himself over the coals for the construction site business.

The second cop also pushed his way in, so that all three stood crowded into the tiny hallway. While Schreub eyeballed Miguel with his worst cop-show intimidation routine, his colleague took out an iPad and opened it to take notes.

"Now, then, kid," Schreub began, "suppose you tell us all about your involvement in this arson attack with your buddy Jade?"

¡Madre purísima! They were like bad copies of the worst actors on cop shows. And he had always thought those programs were so fake. Stubborn, though—he had to give them that.

"Honestly, officer," he tried to convince Schreub, "the last time Jade and I saw each other was three and a half weeks ago, when I'd just got back from the hospital with this." He waved his cast. "That morning she left to go surfing. Obviously, I couldn't go with her, unless I just wanted to sit on the beach like some useless idiot."

But the questions continued. Half an hour later, the officers left, but not before making him understand in no uncertain terms that they didn't believe a word of anything he'd said regarding his innocence or his ignorance of Jade's whereabouts.

"We'll be seeing each other real soon, kid. Remember, you lie to us, and it'll be worse for you when we find out—and we will. Have a nice day!"

He watched them get into their car and drive away. Almost immediately, another car pulled up: Jade's family's battered station wagon. Her stepfather, Patrick, jumped out.

"Miguel! Hi!"

It was feeling like one of those days, and he hadn't even had his cornflakes yet.

"Hi, Mr.... Patrick." Jade's hippie parents were the worst in making all her friends call them by their first names. He felt sorry for her.

"Um, Mr.... I mean, Patrick, I don't know where she is, honest."

"Miguel"—he barged past. What was it with adults? "We need to talk."

"Sure."

Miguel followed Patrick into his living room, dreading what he would hear. Jade's stepdad perched on the edge of the sofa, watching the TV, where the news about Mauri Cove was running again. His eyes didn't leave the screen as he asked:

"You've seen this?"

Well, yeah, the TV is on. There's a good possibility I was watching it before half of Mauri Cove began barging into my living room. But out loud he said, "Yes, I have. Is Jade somehow involved?"

"I was hoping you could enlighten me. This is no time to be protecting her, Miguel. I need to make sure she's safe."

At that, Miguel felt a coldness plummet down his spine.

"All I know is what I've just seen on TV. What happened?"

"It's all a complete mess. Her mom's at the hospital with Kyle. You know about Kyle?"

"Yeah, I mean, I came down to the beach just after you guys left the other day, so I heard. I've been meaning to come around, but thought you guys wouldn't want crowds turning up on your doorstep. I didn't know he was in the hospital."

"He is. He got caught in some poisonous substance out in the bay, and he's ... well, he isn't too good."

"I'm sorry—but how is Jade tied up with that fire?"

Patrick placed his head in his hands. Miguel was afraid the man was about to cry. In that case Miguel had no idea what he would do. But Patrick just sighed and continued:

"Jade was out at the time we had to take Kyle to the hospital, so I waited for her—and she returned late with this ... some sort of foreign orphan boy in tow. He ended up spending the night, and while I was asleep, they both disappeared. I woke up to this ... disaster! Apparently, they were seen around the laboratory and running away from it, escaping in a canoe."

"¡Madre mía!" Trust Jade to complicate an already complicated situation. Patrick turned from the TV and looked at him directly.

"Miguel, I need you to help me find her. You know where she would go, what her haunts are. You and I could look for her together and get to the bottom of this. And we have to do this fast. Her mom is at her wits' end, and Kyle is ... in a serious condition."

"Yes, of course, Mr.... Patrick. I'll do whatever it takes. Don't worry, we'll find her."

Now it was Miguel's turn to sigh. His day suddenly had an objective, but what a tough call!

Morning sunlight glinted off the waves. Though choppy out here, the swell was a good height and nicely spaced for some relaxed morning surfing inshore—for those not wearing a cast.

"That's it."

Patrick pointed ahead, his other hand on the tiller of the dinghy's outboard as it guided them over the bay. Miguel squinted into the sun and saw the three tall towers that he had observed so often from the beach, or when paddling his board out into Mauri Cove, but had never really wondered about.

"It's supposed to be a research station."

"Like the one that was torched?"

"That was the inshore installation, mainly a laboratory, I think. But this is where they were seen to be heading. It's the only place they could have ended up unless they ... unless they capsized."

"Easier to search now, anyway," Miguel noted. "That storm is gone."

It was true. The tornado-like storm that had been

persisting off Mauri Cove for what seemed like weeks had suddenly lifted, and the day was clear and bright. But those towers… something about them Miguel had never liked. Now, what with Jade's disappearance and everything, they looked quite ominous.

"But why would they go there?"

"Jade was very angry at what had happened to her brother. Maybe she thought this research station was involved somehow. But I can't imagine her going as far as to put the whole installation out of business—not arson."

"Well, Kyle got sick from some sort of slick out on the sea; she might have thought that station was respon-sible. Why else would they go there? Though wouldn't they try and hide until the dust settled?"

"Where would they go, Miguel? This whole coast is being scoured. There aren't that many places to hide."

Patrick was staring at him hard. Miguel knew that look. He knew Patrick wasn't going to give up. He sighed. What a morning! It wasn't even eleven o'clock, and here he was sitting out in the middle of Mauri Cove in a tiny dinghy, on a manhunt—or girlhunt.

He sighed again. He would have to tell.

"There is one place, but you can't get there till low tide."

He looked behind them, back toward the coast, which looked brightly scrubbed in the morning sun-light, the cliffs glowing like chalk. His eyes searched them until he spied the vertical shadow about halfway along and down toward the waterline, a triangular patch of dark.

3.
HOSPITALITY

While Kreh-ursh was carried off by his people, Jade remained in the beached canoe. Kreh-otchaw-oh's hull was black-ened from fire and stained by that toxic slime. Yet Jade did not know what else to do. She felt so completely marooned in this world, and had no idea what had happened to her. Was this science or magic? Here she was, cut off totally from her own dimension, with absolutely no passage back. The huddle of huts she could see farther up the beach appeared alien and hostile; she had no wish to approach them.

When the people—mainly children really, though with a few old people in their midst—had taken Kreh-ursh, they had stared—not with any particular malice, but not overly friendly either. It wasn't the sort of hospitality she might have expected from an island people, no serenading her with garlands or their island songs. These people seemed to see her almost as a danger, or the bearer of some threat that she couldn't place.

She had been sitting, head bowed, staring at the canoe's bilges for several minutes when she felt herself observed. Looking up, she spied a gaggle of children of varying ages crouched in hiding behind the closest canoes. Their eyes, studying her, were dark and wary, yet inquisitive, too. Several long moments passed as they observed each other. Then a presence, approaching from the village, made her turn her head: It was the green-eyed girl with the scar—her rescuer. The girl walked up and held out her hand. She didn't seem particularly friendly, but at least she was making contact. She gestured to Jade to follow her.

Jade grabbed her rucksack from the canoe, and she and the girl walked up the beach. Numerous villagers appeared and shadowed them, keeping several yards' respectful—or wary—distance. They were dressed in a similar way to Kreh-ursh, in short, sleeveless tunics of beige, brown, or green. She glimpsed a few old people too, but wondered where the other adults were. Jade and the girl entered among the huts, which were thatch roofed, each in its own fenced compound. It was a large settlement, stretching around the wide sweep of the bay. Finally they stopped at one hut, which appeared to be the girl's own. Three boys, one aged about seven and two identical twins of around eleven—the girl's brothers, she assumed—surrounded their sister, chattering and asking questions. Even considering how alienated Jade felt at having been thrust into this bizarre world, she picked up a disjointed feel to their conversation, as if half the talk were occurring on some mental plane Jade could not access—for she had been unable to re-ignite the limited mind speech she had achieved with Kreh-ursh. They all stared at Jade with round blank eyes, and kept well back, as if she might contaminate them with some disease.

The green-eyed girl indicated that she wait—not in the hut, but outside in the compound—while she disappeared inside. The youngest boy remained, hugging the doorpost. He did not take his eyes off Jade even to blink. Soon the green-eyed girl returned, bearing a mat, a length of cloth and a clay jar in her arms. She laid the jar on top of the mat in front of her and indicated that Jade should sit. Jade cleared her throat. She had had enough of this silence.

"Jade ... Jade. Jaa ... chuu ... naw Jade ... jaan."

The girl reacted in mild surprise before smiling, as if she realized she had been impolite:

"Hoh-ee, Jeh-eed. Jaa chuunaw Geh-meer jaan."

"Hoh-ee, Geh-meer."

Jade felt that soft mind-tap that Kreh-ursh had used, as if the other girl were probing, testing whether she could communicate that way. But Jade could not connect with this girl as she had been able to with Kreh-ursh. It was all too strange. Cut off from every single familiar thing she knew—Mauri Cove, her mom, Kyle, Patrick, Miguel, anybody who spoke her own language—she would have known such mind speech was rubbish had she not already talked with Kreh-ursh that way.

She sat on the mat, feeling suddenly very tired. Geh-meer gestured again, so Jade was about to slip off her t-shirt but felt inhibited by the boys; the twins had joined their younger brother at the doorway and also stared in their silent way. Geh-meer rapped something, and they disappeared into the hut. Jade realized that the girl had read her thought, but was grateful. The other girl waved her up, picked up the mat and jar, and moved farther into the compound, out of view of the hut doorway. There Jade eased off her t-shirt and tattered board shorts, sitting back down on the mat in just her underpants. Maybe it wasn't consider-ed strange here to reveal one's body in front of others. She was an alien in this village, after all. Who knew what was considered normal?

Geh-meer removed the lid of the jar, and Jade submitted while the other girl slathered ointment onto her arms, legs, and neck, covering all her burns and scratches in a thick, pale green cream. It stung at first. Then it burned in a dull sort of way before giving way to a numbing, refreshing sensation. Geh-meer picked up a length of light cloth, similar to muslin, and wrapped it loosely about Jade toga style, taking care not to rub off the cream.

Once she had finished her ministrations, Geh-meer gave a sharp cry, and the two older boys emerged from the hut bearing platters of food. They must have been pre-paring it while Geh-meer was applying her first aid. There were grains cooked with fruit and spices, cold meat, steamed fish and vegetables. The family, and Jade—she had seen no sign of any parents—sat and began to eat. Jade was starving. Compared to the last meal she had eaten —Patrick's mushy tomato sandwiches—this was delicious. She wolfed down the food.

4.
OUT ON THE
WATER

They approached the cave from the north, hugging the coast as close as they dared because the tide was full, and waves crashed onto the rocks below the cliffs.

"They can't have hidden in there," Patrick decided. "Look at that swell and those breakers. They would have been smashed to pieces."

"When the tide's low, you can get in around the rocks. There's a sort of path. That's how Jade and I found it."

"But what time were they spotted? Around seven-forty? This morning's tide was around nine-forty. It would have been way too high. And look at that sea. No boat could get in there."

Miguel had to agree. Patrick turned the dinghy northward again.

"I say we scour the coast, and then have a closer look at that research facility. It's our best bet."

A couple of hours later, they had covered the entire coast for a couple of miles both north and south of Mauri Cove but had found no sign of Jade, the stranger, or any wreckage that might have belonged to any canoe. Miguel, who still hadn't had anything to eat, was starving, but he knew better than to suggest to Jade's stepfather that they head in to grab lunch. Police launches and other craft were also out searching, but Patrick and Miguel felt a certain hostility each time they came close to another vessel. The searchers recognized Patrick as Jade's guardian. It was clear they were blaming her for the arson attack.

"Okay, I'm curious about that research facility," said Patrick.

"But we won't be allowed on there, will we?"

"I don't intend to ask permission. If Jade's out there, I'm going to find her. You can feel these people's attitude —they're angry about that fire. It's under-standable: People were relying on Synengine to create jobs. So we have to find Jade before they do."

Patrick turned the dinghy's bow seaward once again. Miguel looked around, checking the positions of the other craft, but they were all far away at other points across the bay or up and down the coast. The direction that their small dinghy was taking went unnoticed.

As they approached the towers again, Miguel was able to observe them more closely than he ever had. The three pillars thrust up from the sea in a triangular formation, their smooth concrete bright in the morning sun. Crowning each pillar was a wide, flat platform, alongside a thin bronze spire, which tapered up to a gleaming point far above. While the expanse of sea stretching between the pillars was the size of several football fields, the towers were linked by what appeared to be narrow suspension bridges, each one consisting of a single long span. As they approached the nearest pillar, they saw that bolted to it at sea level was a metal dock, large enough to moor a good-sized motor vessel, painted a glaring rescue orange, which stood out angrily against the green sea. Another construction, which looked like an elevator shaft, rose from the dock to the height of the suspension bridges. The entire complex had a megalithic and impersonal air.

Miguel felt increasingly intimidated the closer they approached. As if to confirm his unease, he could see uniformed figures manning the dock.

"How would Jade have got on there, past those guards?"

Out here on the open sea, he had to shout above the wind to make Patrick hear him, but the installation's imposing size seemed to demand a silence that made him feel he was challenging it. Patrick, too, appeared at a loss.

"We'll take a look at the other two towers," he decided. "You never know."

Patrick took the dinghy in a wide arc around the nearest tower and headed for the one that was sited the farthest seaward. Miguel became more and more awestruck.

"These are humungous—some research station! This is more like an oil rig, like a nuclear power plant."

"And how did they get these constructions erected out here without us really noticing? We knew they were building something, but nothing on this scale!"

"Must be pretty big experiments they're doing."

It took them over ten minutes' chugging along in the dinghy to get close to the next tower, which gave them a sense of just how huge the construction was. At first glance, this tower seemed identical to the first: the monolithic concrete column rising from the waves, connected by long bridges to the other towers; the bright orange dock and an elevator shaft rising to bridge height. Yet the elevator on this pillar terminated in a wide platform that ringed the entire construction. Angled plate-glass windows high up showed what looked like lighted offices or laboratories installed on top.

"I'd say that was the head office," Patrick called above the sound of the wind. "If Jade came out here, this would be the tower she'd pick to go on board, I'm sure of it."

They could see uniformed guards stationed on the docks. Whether they were there for security or operational reasons was anybody's guess, but Miguel doubted they would allow Patrick and Miguel to dock without authorization. Miguel was beginning to feel that this search was getting out of hand. There was no sign of Jade and no evidence whatsoever that she had tried to get onto this installation, legally or otherwise.

"Patrick? I can't see how Jade could have hidden anywhere around here. My guess is that she's holed up in that cave. If we go back now, when the tide drops, we can be the first ones to go in and get her."

Patrick looked at him for a long moment, as if trying to determine whether the boy was lying to him. Then he nodded.

"You're right—though if she isn't there, I think we'll

have to explore this possibility. Let's head back by way of the third tower, just in case she's clinging to a spar or something."

They turned the dinghy and headed for the final tower.

5.
RETURN HOME

Rrehn-ursh threw his paddle into the air and laughed. Working on a raft of canoes on the remotest edge of the lagoon, near Zjhuud-geh's reef, he had picked up the far-flung thought message earlier than anyone. People immediately mind-asked, wanting to know what he had heard, but he jumped straight into his canoe, cast off, and headed for the beach.

With his contingent, Rrehn-ursh had been assigned to try to clean up the death stain that had all but destroyed Zjhuud-geh, the Sacred Isle. Before the storm, this island had been the brightest jewel in the entire ocean of Shah, where generations of his people had been coming to complete the rite by which they became adults of the tribe of the Shahee, or sea nomads. This lagoon—of what used to be clear azure waters brimming with corals, fish, and other sea life, lapping at the fine white sands of its pristine beaches — was now sealed with a thick, dark sludge, a poison that had killed every living thing on the reef. The sea life was dead, and the beaches had turned to gray mud. This was the death that had been brought through the rift.

Yet all this destruction could not dampen Rrehn-ursh's spirits. Raising his voice in a clear chant, he whipped up wind and waves to propel his canoe in the way of his people, sending the craft pushing through the ooze toward the beach. Other Shahee, out of mindshot, looked up at his haste, wondering what news he had heard. Though tempted to mind-shout, he preferred to give his news face to face. For—though delicate—it was good news.

His friend was working with a team of Shahee scraping black mud off the beach sand and shoveling it into a huge pile above the high tide mark. Who knew what they would do with it after that?

"Kehdurn!"

His friend turned and, leaning on his wooden shovel, awaited Rrehn-ursh's approach. He knew something had occurred but not what, so he stood there, expectant. Rrehn-ursh wanted to break the news cautiously, but he couldn't keep from smiling. So Kehdurn at least knew the tidings were not bad.

"They're alive! They came back through!"

He meant the rift, that bizarre mix of tornado and whirlpool that had spirited two young people—Kehdurn's son and Rrehn-ursh's daughter—from their village into the ether. Kreh-ursh and Geh-meer had left their village as non-adults, candidates in the rite that would confirm them as sea nomads and full members of their tribe. But they had not returned to their village. In mid-seas, the elder, the shahiroh Taashou, had instructed Kreh-ursh that he must seek out the cause of the floating black islands that were poisoning their sea. So Kreh-ursh, shunning the celebration of adulthood that awaited him in his village, had paddled his canoe into the whirlpool rift and been swallowed by the place from where the poison came. After he had been missing for several days, Rrehn-ursh's daughter Geh-meer, barely confirmed as a full adult, had defied her elders and also swum alone into the terrifying rift. Since that moment, the two young people had been as if dead.

As Rrehn-ursh looked at his friend, the haggard mask that Kehdurn had worn since Kreh-ursh's disappearance seemed to melt away. He sighed, tears welling up even as he laughed.

"I can't believe it! I thought ... I'd never see him again."

But Rrehn-ursh had to say something, to warn his friend.

"He is alive, Kehdurn, but ..."

"What?"

Rrehn-ursh huffed.

"He's been badly burned ... his entire body, especially his back. He's at your home. Your wife's nursing him. He's ... He's back in our world, Kehdurn. Geh-meer brought him back ... and they think he's going to live."

Kehdurn looked at him, realizing that Rrehn-ursh was saying his son might die. He began running along the beach toward his canoe, Rrehn-ursh in pursuit.

"We'll go together," Rrehn-ursh panted. "I have to see Geh-meer."

Between them, they launched the canoe into the flat water of the lagoon and jumped aboard. Kehdurn took the senior, rear position since it was his vessel. Like most of the other Shahee craft, the outer hull was discolored with the black material from the rift. Smudges stained the interior, as well.

"I didn't want him to go.... I knew it might be his path ... I just had a feeling.... You know, after what happened to his friend Kaar-oh ... I began to see him differently. He'll always be my son, but ... I got this feeling about his future.... I thought he was too young for the sea-nomad-becoming.... But to go through that ... thing! How could Taashou have thought.... She's brutal, Rrehn. It's like she's so obsessed with the life code, she doesn't care about people's lives."

"Well, forget about that for now, mate. He's back, he's alive, and he'll be on his feet again in no time. Come on, concentrate. By combining our chanting we might make it home in a day."

6.
THE CAVE

When the wash of each wave no longer touch-ed the lowest rocks, leaving their green beards of weed fully exposed, Miguel judged the time was right. He set off around the cliffs, sloshing knee-deep through the tide. It was just before three.

After the boat excursion—since the tide had been too high to explore the cave, and they couldn't get on board the towers—Patrick and Miguel had headed in to shore. Patrick, having received a call from Jade's mom as they were beaching the dinghy, had arranged to meet her at the hospital. Miguel, thankful to be rescued from chaperoning Patrick around Mauri Cove, now had a freer rein to explore: He thought he'd have a better chance of tracking down Jade on his own. He was also keen to find her before the adults did, to help her should she need it.

After he had been skirting around the headland beneath the lighthouse for twenty minutes, the water below the rocks became too deep for wading. Knowing that meant the tide had already turned—while he was still a fair distance from the cave—he increased his pace. But now he had to clamber over the boulders at the base of the cliffs, so his progress was slower.

That time they had found the cave, he recalled, it had also been a race against the sea. If he remembered right, they had come across it about halfway around to the next cove, and after exploring it for barely ten minutes, they had noticed the tide rising again. Rather than heading on to the far beach—a destination they might not have been able to reach—they had retraced their steps. Even so, the final half mile back to Mauri Cove had been fraught with danger, with huge waves crashing over the rocks, drenching them and making every foothold treacherously slippery.

Despite his haste, as he neared the cave, Miguel saw that the green-bearded rocks were now under water. He would need to be brief and convincing in his arguments to get Jade to return with him in time—if he found her—or they might both get trapped. Possibly the entire cave became submerged at each high tide, in which case, if Jade had trusted to hiding out here…. Yet he seemed to remember a dry shelf of rock above the sea's highest reaches. *Que sea así.* Let it be so, he prayed.

Coming around a rocky outcrop, he spied it. From down on the rocks it looked as high as a cathedral, like a sacred nave vertically piercing the cliff face. Listening, he could hear no voice or movement except the ever present crashing of surf.

"Jade!"

His was the only voice that echoed from the cave's

depths. He called again, but still no response. To the right was the rocky ledge he and Jade had inched their way up, and he went toward it. If Jade was here, she was obviously hiding, scared of being apprehended by the police or falling into Rena's vengeful clutches.

He pressed himself to the cliff wall and eased his way along the ledge, making sure he placed his feet securely one after the other as he edged his way into the cave. Below him, even at low tide, the ocean churned and exploded in its spumy gulch. If he slipped and fell, he knew his hope of survival would be slim. His feeling of relief was huge as he stepped onto the relative safety of the rear platform.

Here the only thing he could hear was the boom and crash of the ocean, echoing back on itself end-lessly. He surveyed the space, but it appeared empty. Clearly, Jade was not here: This had been a wild goose chase. Still, he walked to and fro, exploring. As his eyes adjusted to the gloom, he noticed scuff marks on the rock floor. Crouching to examine them, he could see that something heavy had been dragged across it recently. Yet looking over the lip of the ledge, he knew it was impossible for any craft to have landed here. Even at high tide, the water would be simply too treacherous. A log must have washed up here and been rolled and scraped in a recent spring tide.

Turning to go, anxious to beat the rising tide, he glanced around the cavern a final time. One particular stone caught his eye. Smooth and brown, it appeared more like a wave-polished boulder from the deep, rounded in the surf, than the jagged outcroppings of this cliff face. Then he realized: It wasn't a boulder. He walked over and picked it up. It was a finely carved gourd. A leather thong was attached to it so it could be carried on a belt, and it had a stopper inserted near the stem for using as a container for liquids. Though it was empty, the carvings across its surface were so beautiful and strange that Miguel knew he had to keep it. Maybe he would take it to a museum and find out if it was very old.

But there was something else. Next to where the gourd had lain, a depression in the rock had filled with sand. Bang in its center was the perfect, fresh imprint of a human foot. Miguel dropped to his knees. It had to be Jade's, but did she have such big feet? Then he got another surprise: Scrunched into the sand at the base of the footprint—almost buried—was a small, red leather pouch. Miguel picked it up and opened it. A delicately carved wooden shape slid into his hands, the most beautiful thing he had ever seen. Its fluid lines seemed to follow the grain of the wood as if it had grown into that form, almost as if it were alive. He returned it to its pouch and hung it around his neck as if that were the most natural action in the world. He would keep this. It must contain an answer somehow. Yet the tide was rising. He had to leave.

7.
SPEAK TO ME!

You'll be all right. You'll pull through."

Jade's voice boomed in the small hut, and, though she tried to sound convincing, it rang hollow to her ears—as if her language somehow clashed with the way this world was put together. Yet she needed some sound she recognized: her own words in her own language. That was about all she had here, having floated around in a bubble of silence for over a day now. Her words grounded her, offering a sense of reality, some proof that this was not a dream. So she didn't care if no one understood.

Even her clothes were no longer her own. She was dressed in a simple brown tunic belonging to Geh-meer, her own shorts and t-shirt having been badly burned in the fire. Using a piece of leather, she had belted the tunic tightly, trying to make it look less like a dress, but she wasn't satisfied.

Kreh-ursh lay on a mat under which some sort of

fern leaves had been placed for cushioning, in an alcove off the main space of his hut. Jade was squatting on the hard earth floor beside him. He was lying face down, as he had fewer burns on his front, his head turned toward her and carefully positioned so he could breathe freely. And his entire body had been slathered in the same thick paste Geh-meer had applied to Jade the evening before and that morning.

Looking down at this boy-man, Jade felt that he was her oldest and dearest friend—in fact, here, in this world, he was. Yet she knew nothing about him. They had met barely two days before.

Though still feeling tender, she herself was greatly recovered. The night had been long and uncomfortable. Only her exhaustion had allowed her to sleep at all, since her burns stopped her from rolling over or moving around much. Yet this morning, she felt refreshed and noted with surprise that her skin already seemed to be healing. The ointment had been absorbed, and, while the burns were slightly puffed up, they had taken on a moist, glowing appearance, as if her skin had begun to regenerate.

The same could not be said of Kreh-ursh. His burns were deep and harsh. Parts of his body were nothing but naked flesh, seared black and scarlet, and most of his skin was yellow from the flames. She could see that it would take far more than a miracle cream to heal his wounds.

"That ointment that your friend Geh-meer applied ... it's good. You'll be better in no time."

She felt silly, talking to an unconscious person, but she had heard that it was good to keep speaking to people when they were in a coma. That thought reminded her of Kyle, and she wished she had talked to him more while she was at the hospital.

In another part of the hut she could sense rather than see Kreh-ursh's mother. When Jade had first entered, his mother had been seated beside him, but she had withdrawn into the shadows at Jade's arrival. His father was away. Along with most of the village, he had gone to fight some sort of disaster. It annoyed her to feel the mother's continual probing at her mind, but she tried not to show it. She might be the woman's only link to her son's present condition, and Jade knew that if the positions were reversed, she would probably do the same. His mother was merely trying to solve the mystery for herself. Everyone used that sort of mental communication here.

Kreh-ursh's breathing was the only sound, a barely discernible rasping in the stillness. For some reason it made her think of that ghost who had saved her in the water, the same spirit that had possessed her brother. It was an enigma she could not fathom: How could such an insubstantial spirit have saved her? Yet at the time it had felt real, the way it had pulled her out from under the burning slick, and whispered the words, *Ee-kawg-zjhur ... the jewel fish, for Kai-al-lee ... for Kreh-ursh ...! You are now their only hope.* What did that mean?

Geh-meer appeared in the doorway. She looked at Jade but seemed simultaneously to be in silent communication with Kreh-ursh's mother, for as she entered, the other woman appeared from the rear of the hut, and they both knelt beside Jade. The three of them stayed there silently for several minutes. Jade felt that the two other women were communing with each other, or possibly trying to reach Kreh-ursh, and she wished she could do the same. She stretched her mind out, seeking for the mental speech she and Kreh-ursh had enjoyed at the laboratory, but she felt no contact at all.

The only thing she had to offer was what the ghost in the water had given her. And though she had no idea of its significance, she had to try.

"Geh-meer ... ee-kawg-zjhur."

She hoped she had said it right. Geh-meer turned to her with a quizzical expression. Kreh-ursh's mother glanced at her, almost with scorn, before returning her attention to her son.

"Ee-kawg ... zjhur.... What ... is it?" Jade asked.

Geh-meer reached out and hugged Kreh-ursh's mother gently. She looked down at Kreh-ursh for a moment, then abruptly stood up and, gesturing for Jade to follow, ducked out of the hut. Jade, unsure what to do, offered Kreh-ursh's mother a tentative handshake, but the woman recoiled as if Jade had slapped her. Feeling tears welling at that simple rejection, Jade followed Geh-meer from the hut.

8.
A SENSE OF LOSS

J oan looked down at a half-eaten meat pie that sat leathery and abandoned on her plate. Patrick sighed and took a sip of tea.

"I don't know what can have got into her."

"I do," Joan was grim. "That boy, wherever he's from."

Officer Schreub put away his iPad, drained his cup, and scraped back his chair.

"Well, I don't need to stress to you both that this is serious. As her legal guardians, you're both responsible. In view of your son's delicate condition, we'll tread lightly. But as soon as young Jade shows up, you are legally required to inform the police. Is that clear?"

"Yes, officer, my wife's a lawyer. We know what the legal ramifications of this are."

"Well, it's all written down here on this paper, just in case anyone gets any short-term memory loss. I'll get an autograph on my copy from you both if you don't mind.... Thanks."

"Thank you, officer. We'll be in touch as soon as she turns up."

"I hope your son gets well, folks. I'll be in contact."

"Well," hissed Patrick angrily once the policeman had left the hospital cafeteria, "What in heck has the young idiot got herself into this time?"

"Leave it, Pat. It's my fault. I was stressing with Kyle. I've been short with her, haven't given her the attention she needed."

"It is not your fault, dear! She knows this is a difficult time, and she's old enough to know when she needs to pull her weight ... and this! Darling, she's blown up a building! That's thousands of millions of dollars.... We couldn't come up with a couple of thousand even to repair its front gates.... And we're legally responsible!"

"I know, but let's concentrate on priorities: Forget the money for now and think of the people. One of us has to stay with Kyle, and one of us has to find Jade ... fast."

"You stay with Kyle. I'll keep looking for Jade."

"Are you sure, Pat? She doesn't need a tirade right now. I know Jade. She'll be feeling bad enough as it is. If you blast off a broadside at her, she's likely to burn *our* house down, too. You'd best sit with Kyle, and I'll go and look for her."

"I'm not going to roast her, I promise ... much as I'm tempted. I just haven't got a clue where to keep looking. Miguel and I searched the entire bay. It's like she's just vanished."

"Well, the watchman said they escaped in a small speedboat—you can probably add that to your list of stolen or damaged goods—but she could have got a long way up the coast in that."

"The coast guards have been scouring the region for

hours now. There's no sign of her. Would she have headed up here, toward the city?"

"We can't give up, Pat. She's my daughter. I must find her."

"Okay, I'll keep looking. I'll call you on your cell...."

"You can't. It got drenched while we were out rescuing Kyle. Call me on the phone up at the ward. Here's the number."

She passed him the card that the hospital had given her.

"Shall we go up and see Kyle? I want to see the little man before I get back to the search."

Joan sighed. "There's no change. He isn't any worse, but he's still in a coma."

"I want to see him, all the same."

Kyle, a boy of nine, lay unmoving on the hospital bed. The machines and screens that surrounded him kept his heart beating and forced his lungs to inflate with air, feeding oxygen to his brain. Patrick sat beside his bed and held his hand as he told him one of the stories he'd always loved. It concerned a fisherman alone on the sea, who cast his line into the waves and caught the fisher king's daughter.

"She rose through the depths, her silver limbs wrapped about his line, his iron hook caught deep in her breast."

Though Kyle had always loved the story, it also

frightened him.

"Didn't she bleed to death from the fisherman's hook?" he would ask.

"No, she lived. But because the hook had pierced her heart, and was made from the stoutest iron in the land, it left a hole that never healed, so no more could she frolic in the surf or return to her kingdom beneath the waves. For if she did, she would drown."

Deep inside his coma, the part of Kyle that might have responded to this story could not hear the words. But his heart latched on to the deep rumble of his stepfather's voice as he lay cocooned, captive within his own body. Unable to make out the words, he could still hear the love, and would have surged to the surface, to wakefulness, to hug his stepfather, had he been able.

Above and around him hovered another presence, nebulous, like a red mist. This alien spirit had entered his mind as he lay sick, and taken control. Kyle did not have the strength to fight it.

Some time earlier, that vaporous presence had withdrawn for a space. Kyle's mind had followed, carried on the back of the mist the way a cripple might be carried across a river in a flood. He was in a world of jade, a deep, green, underwater world. Then he saw his sister. She was sleeping on the bed of a river or lake, looking pale and peaceful. But they were pulling her up, the mist surrounding her, and Kyle was carried along within it. They strove to wake her. An instant later, the water turned into fire and everything became red-orange, billowing up through the water toward the air. Flames danced on the surface as Jade vomited in the shallows. Then they were once more withdrawing, and he was back, captive again in his own body with the red presence pressed heavily on top of him. That was all he knew until, after a long period of stillness, he perceived this rumbling attempt by his stepfather to reach him. He knew also that the ruby miasma was not aware that he had traveled on its back to the river, or that he had reached out to Jade.

A nd finally, though he knew she was going to her death for the sake of one last glimpse of her childhood home, the fisherman was forced to let his beloved wife slip away. For he loved her so much, he could not deny her one last wish."

Patrick felt Joan's hand on his shoulder as he finished. He took it and held it. Kyle remained unmoving.

"I'll stay with him now, Pat. Please, try and find Jade."

Patrick stood and hugged his wife.

"Don't worry, I'll find her."

They kissed. Then Joan sat down beside her son, and Patrick left the ward.

9.
KENZ-OH

own on the beach, Geh-meer stood looking out over the bay. Jade came down the sand. As she approached, Geh-meer turned and looked at her. Jade felt the other's mind presence and knew what was coming. If they were to help Kreh-ursh, if she had any hope of ever returning to help her brother, she must break this silence in which she was immersed. She needed to be able to talk to the people of this world, to overcome their hostility, and convince them that she wanted to help.

Together they walked along the beach, to where a low promontory of rocks projected into the bay. Geh-meer led the way, stepping from rock to rock till they reached a large, flat boulder surrounded by water. There they sat down facing each other. Having undergone a similar process with Kreh-ursh, Jade knew what to expect, and she allowed Geh-meer to place her hands on her temples. Jade tried to relax her mind, to become as open as she could to the other girl's mind.

She was unprepared for the forcefulness of Geh-meer's mental touch when it came. There was that charge of something like white noise; then she felt the other inside her head, showing her images just like Kreh-ursh had done. Again she saw the village of Rrurd, though now that she was physically here, it seemed so much clearer than the vision Kreh-ursh had shared with her. She saw Geh-meer's family: her father, who was away fighting the floating death, and her brothers, as well as other people in the village. She recognized the scary old woman who had sent Kreh-ursh on his mission into her world. With a shock she saw the gap-toothed boy, the ghost who had saved her in the river. But here he was, seemingly alive and laughing, friends with Geh-meer and Kreh-ursh as they trained for sea-nomad-becoming. There was the island where Geh-meer and Kreh-ursh—the other boy no longer with them—had undertaken their ritual.

Though Geh-meer tried to shield it, Jade understood, finally, the depth of the girl's attachment to Kreh-ursh. Then and there she vowed not to step between them. Not that she had ever been particularly interested in dating, anyway. The way that the other girls in her school primped and preened and fell about, desperate to attract the boys' attention, had always seemed to her slightly pathetic. Perhaps that was why she had always felt more comfortable with boys as friends. Darren and Miguel didn't expect her to be anything she wasn't; they just treated her like one of themselves—almost. And she thought of Kreh-ursh as a friend, too, nothing more. Sure, she could see he was handsome and strong in a rough sort of a way, but she was hardly about to go all girlish and quivery. Geh-meer was welcome to him.

She was surprised at Geh-meer's feelings, though, as she respected the older girl. Since meeting her, she had seen the other do what needed to be done swiftly and with no fuss. She was tough, talented, and capable. Jade liked that about her and wanted her approval.

But Geh-meer was pulling her attention back to a vision of the slick spewing forth from the tornado that had brought her here. And, as Kreh-ursh had shown her, she saw the devastation that the black stain was causing in this world. It was the same substance that had made Kyle sick, the gunk from the laboratory. Well, it was over—the laboratory was no more. The priority now was to clean up the mess and save Kyle and Kreh-ursh. She had to tell Geh-meer that.

The vision lifted. They were seated together on the rock facing each other. This was fine, but not what Jade wanted. What she needed was to be able to talk, to communicate with Geh-meer. She tried the mind speech:

Can you hear me?

Geh-meer seemed puzzled that Jade had drawn back. Once again she let a stream of images flow into Jade's mind, but no words. Frustrated, Jade wanted to pull away again, but something compelled her to focus. The vision showed an underwater scene. An ephemeral creature shone brightly, its lithe form slipping through the green depths, colored scales flashing. As soon as she focused on it, it disappeared, but that brief vision burned itself deep into her consciousness.

"Ee-kawg-zjhur?" she asked in words. Her only hope was to repeat the question she had asked in the hut, in the hope it might spark some inspiration in Geh-meer.

She opened her eyes to find Geh-meer looking at her, but when Jade tried to push a thought of her own toward Geh-meer—*What is it?*—the girl turned and looked out over the water, thinking. She seemed not to have heard.

Jade looked back at the beach, thinking of Kyle. The full weight of her failure now struck her. Trapped in this world, she knew her brother would die, while she could do nothing. Geh-meer's gaze returned to her, and Jade knew she was sifting her thoughts. Yet Jade could not understand, could not say what she wanted!

Geh-meer stood up, her mind as unreadable as ever, and motioned to Jade to follow her, nodding shore-ward. Jade had no idea what they might do next, but followed her companion, and they began hopping back across the rocks to the beach. Imagining that they would return to sit with Kreh-ursh, to try to help him heal, she was surprised when Geh-meer turned in another direction through the village.

They walked between the huts, gradually approach-ing the center of Rrurd. It was a large village. Quite suddenly they came out into a large open space. In the center, a wide, spreading tree cast its branches low. Geh-meer walked toward it. Following her, Jade saw that in its shade, leaning against its massive roots and even seated on its thick boughs were children of all ages up to about twelve years old. They were listening to an old man who was sitting on an exposed root.

Geh-meer and Jade sat down on the ground at the rear of the enthralled assembly and waited for the old man to finish. His story came out as a singing chant, words rising, rumbling up from his belly in a rhythmical meter. Never quite constant, the verses flowed and ebbed like the tide, according to the action. Jade listened mesmerized, though understanding nothing of his speech. Finally, he seemed to come to a conclusion, and waved the children away.

That was when they became aware of Jade and surrounded her, their intense, dark eyes seeming to hem her in with the hypnotic power of their curiosity. Geh-meer snapped something, both mentally and verbally, and they scattered, running off in all directions around the village.

"Tehl chuunaw Kenz-oh Tehlaan," Geh-meer introduced.

Jade swallowed and stepped forward.

"Hoh-ee, Kenz-oh. Jaa-chuunaw Jeh-eed-jaan."

Kenz-oh was a tiny, wiry man with a high, domed pate and a wispy beard. Though Jade was standing within a couple of yards of him, he got up from his place and shuffled closer, scrutinizing her with eyes as bright and green as Geh-meer's. He directed a question at Geh-meer, without taking his eyes from Jade. Geh-meer answered in a long and complicated sentence, of which Jade caught only the words "ee-kawg-zjhur." Kenz-oh continued to study Jade for long moments after the girl from Rrurd finished speaking. Then he turned, waving them both away, and shuffled toward a shaded crook under two thick, low-hanging boughs, between which was slung a hammock piled with blankets and cushions.

IO.
MYTH OF THE JEWEL FISH

Geh-meer took the stranger back to the tree that evening. Even though she was now Shahee, the memory of evenings such as this touched a tender chord inside. Little had changed since she used to come here as a child. A low fire burned close to where Kenz-oh's hammock hung from the ancient boughs, shielded by a low barrier of rocks to minimize the danger of sparks rising into the overhanging branches. Rrurd's youngsters had once more congregated around the trunk, taking up their positions on its bulbous roots and low-hanging limbs.

Kenz-oh himself was settled on a boulder close to the fire. In Rrurd, they boasted he was the best wit with words the length and breadth of Shah. Geh-meer still thought so. With a goblet of green zjheh-rohsh wine cupped between his knobby fingers, Kenz-oh stroked his beard and cleared his throat to announce he was ready.

For a moment Geh-meer forgot the stranger, and once again it was she, Kreh-ursh, and Kaar-oh who were sitting between those roots as teenagers, waiting for the old man to spin one of his fantastic tales. Kaar-oh, who had been playing with a stick from the fire — seeing how much of it he could burn without scorching his fingers—threw it back into the embers and snapped at the noisy young ones:

"Sheen-gaw aleef! He's ready!"

Kenz-oh looked around at these children—who were much the same age as she had been all those years ago—with a stern, attention-commanding glare that Geh-meer still found scary, even now that she was full Shahee.

"Let me tell you the myth of Kawg-zjhur, the jewel fish."

He took a breath and, launching into the sing-song tones of the old dialect, began to weave the old words into ever-fresh harmonies.

"I'll sing the story of the Kawg-zjhur, the valiant creature who saved us all, of how she earned all her brilliant colors, that bold wee fighter on a distant morn."

Geh-meer glanced at the stranger. She hoped that somehow Kenz-oh with his skill might be able to penetrate her thick skull, start her communicating. With the rift closed and Kreh-ursh desperately ill, this stranger was the only person who knew the nature of the black stain from her world that was killing the ocean of Shah. They needed her knowledge. And the stranger had seemed to indicate that the myth of the jewel fish was significant, so they had to try. Yet the newcomer was sitting with her head down, eyes closed; there was no sign she understood a thing.

Part of what made Kenz-oh's storytelling so vivid was that he could speak in words and mind speech at the same time. It was a strange combination, like hearing a reverberating echo of words that pierced deeply inside of you. So Geh-meer still hoped the stranger might perceive something, even if only some tiny shred of knowledge. She returned her attention to Kenz-oh.

"You might not call her a hero, or gaudy at all; she was such a plain little fish, dull and faun colored. Fuubh-zjhur, mud fish, they called her. Yet with her tremendous courage and valor, her wit prevailed, and she beat the greatest pterodactyl of them all, the evil and greedy Bhaanj-krraash-oh.

"That morning, Geh-urbh's first born, our forebears, went swimming toward the choppy blue sea, and she swam along, too. Though she struggled to keep up with her tribe, she was small for such rushing waters, and soon was left behind.

"So, tired of traveling, she rested a while. Digging deep into the warm mud of the riverbank, hidden from sight, she gazed out on that new world, on young creation just starting to wake. Alone, and in search of adventure, she was drinking the fresh draught of life for the very first time.

"Unimagined beasts were being awoken back then, the bright verdure of vegetation stirring in that virgin mountain valley, where no fear existed, nor strife. She saw seedlings and flowers bravely sprouting, and forest trunks reaching high, vines twining soft tendrils about them, as they stretched their limbs up into the light.

"Creatures were born, and building nests or roaming, cantering or stalking through the wilds, or swinging themselves aloft into the leafy gloaming, they all explored their new world. Some spread shining wings wide and soared up into air never yet breathed by any living thing.

"The sole creature watching on that dawn, a mute witness to the birth of our tribe—of men and women—was the mud fish, Fuubh-zjhur. Only she saw our mother, Geh-urbh, give slow birth one final time and bring her two most troublesome young out into the light.

"Down the alpine slopes they came gamboling, Teh-ot and Kaa-urbh, those innocent infants already fast growing tall. One day, humans—having grown into their fullest powers—would protect their wild kin, but right then, they played where those twin peaks tower, mindless to peril, beneath an open sky.

"These children even then were honing their skills: Kaa-urbh, the hunter, undefeated, was already notching up her first kills. So it is that some life, recently born, must succumb almost immediately to death. We sacrifice ourselves, and we sacrifice others; this is the nature of the life code, and the balance is maintained; for we are the guardians, but also the fishers; we give our lives for life, and we take life to live.

"Her brother concentrated on rubbing sticks together: one, a fired sapling cut from the bhayd tree, and the other, dried keerr heather bark, both cut from a volcano's morning shade. Make a boat of the keerr and sharpen the bhayd spear within it. Sparks will glow, and smoke will curl, before fire leaps. This is how we make fire, children, and it was Teh-ot's boyhood gift to all of his folk. Fire is still worth more to us than the most precious coral in our lagoon.

"So engrossed were the children that neither felt the swift eclipsing of the bright sun above, how a cool shadow stained the crystal stream dark, rending the sunlight into scattered bits. So intent on their games were the children that they felt not the air turn as chill as a scream, carrying a clatter of quills that clashed with all the perfect creations that had been born that day.

"From out of the sun he dropped, his nostrils blowing fiery billows. When finally—but were they too late?—the twins looked up, they saw, plummeting like a rock from on high, the fell Bhaanj-krraash-oh!

"His wings were taut as leather drumheads stretched across a whale bone, their shadow blotting out the bright day. He exuded a smoking, sulfurous stench, snorting blasts of flame that enwreathed his hideous maw of knife-like fangs. And his talons! If you saw those claws, you would quake! In search of prey he came, yearning for the blood-filled flesh of newborn young, tensed to tear soft flesh, his spiked tail snaking through the air like a hideous monster in its own right— the dragon's weaponry was terrible.

"Worst of all were his eyes! They glowed hypnotically, a traitorous dragon gaze that clove so keen to his prey as never to leave his victim till after death.

"Ah! Had it continued so, neither you nor I nor any human would be here to tell the tale. Our race might have perished and a race of dragons prevailed.

"It is Fuubh-zjhur, that valiant little fish, we have to

thank for our existence. For no sooner did she see the peril than she left her burrow and swam out into the center of the stream where the water flows deep and fast. She swam to the children's aid. Her sole wish was to save those children from being slain.

"Prompted by instincts as yet untried, she drank deep of the rippling waters. She drank and drank until that broad torrent slowed and became a shallow stream. Yet still she sucked up the water course until it trickled dry, and she lay writhing among the mossy boulders, stranded on the bare streambed. No longer a tiny mite was she, but a swollen giant of a fish, and as tempting a prey as a greedy dragon might crave."

With these words, Geh-meer recalled the time, all those years ago, that a single child had broken Kenz-oh's thread:

"I don't believe it."

She remembered the moment well. Nobody interrupted Kenz-oh. Ever. Or almost never. Everyone had looked around to see Kaar-oh staring at Kenz-oh in defiance.

"How could she drink up so much water in such a short space of time, just a few seconds?"

Kenz-oh paused.

"Well ... she had powerful lungs! She was a very special fish, remember. There has never been such a special fish since."

Kenz-oh seemed to think his answer had been accepted by his listeners, but Geh-meer looked across to see Kaar-oh frowning in disapproval. It probably wasn't the first time a child had questioned one of

Kenz-oh's stories, but it was the first time that Geh-meer had seen Kaar-oh, young as he was, defy an adult so boldly. Kenz-oh seemed unaware of the boy's anger, and continued with his story.

"Bhaanj-krraash-oh spied her swollen form, and in his greed swung that flame-wreathed maw her way.

"Could Fuubh-zjhur endure? Would not the dragon seize her and rend her asunder? Was she not doomed to perish in the beast's insides?

"But just at the last, in one mighty blast, Fuubh-zjhur spat out her water with the force of a spear. Up it flew into Bhaanj-krraash-oh's gullet, deep into the fiery furnace.

"With a howl, the worm-spawn fought to rise. But his wing caught a tree and, roaring in anguish, he crashed belly-heavy down onto the bank. His landing shook the earth, and every creature alive felt the moment of his final fall.

"In his agony, as his claws carved canyons, and his tail scythed trees from the ground, water doused the fire in the bhaanj, while vapor hissed and poured from his throat, ears, and eyes. At last, with a shuddering moan, his light went dim. That angry beast fell down and died.

"The twins, stunned to see the spark extinguished, surveyed the corpse. The dragon was dead and lay like a mountain steaming morning mist as smoke arose from the devastation around about. Fuubh-zjhur's force seemed likewise spent. Having chosen to give her fresh life to save the children, she was gasping her last as Teh-ot and Kaa-urbh knelt beside her and wept.

"Yet Kaa-urbh, the huntress, was not one made for grief. Nor would she have that fish expire before her time. Gathering up their waning deliverer, she bore the fish toward the beast. Taking an edge of flint, she rent Bhaanj-krraash-oh's hide and released all the vapor and stink of his foul insides. Smells of sulfur, acid, and ash arose from the corpse, vile in the fresh air of the new world. Yet deep in depths flashing brilliant with every rainbow hue, amid wreaths of steam and noxious gas, a lake so rich in minerals had grown that it became known as the lake of stone. Kaa-urbh released the failing fish into that sparkling loch. And then a brilliant sight occurred: Beneath the surface of those waters, Fuubh-zjhur found new life. She shed her muddy robes forever and was transformed into ee-kawg-zjhur, the jewel fish, a creature containing every pigment that light might reflect. By adopting all those sparkling colors, she became a jewel of myriad hues.

"From the dragon's nostrils a stream began to trickle. We call it Bhaanj-krraash-oh-saan, which means the blood of the dragon. And dragon's blood is a strong cure-all, but beware of drinking there, for Krraash-oh's ghost still haunts that mere, drawing unwary souls into the lake's song with his craving.

"Of course, the tale I'm telling you is a myth and untrue. Nobody has ever seen the great dragon, or the jewel fish. Or if so, they held their secret fast.

"For while you may see below the water's surface calm and learn what I know not, touching the sparkling quartz of the Dragon Belly leads you away to worlds far less sane than our own."

Kenz-oh was silent then. Geh-meer looked at the stranger. She was reclining against one of the tree's large exposed roots, her eyes closed and knees drawn up. Naturally, she couldn't have understood a single word of the story, but Geh-meer couldn't resist brushing her mind gently over the other girl's to feel what she might have received.

Knowing that the stranger was sensitive to mind speech, she tried to be as subtle as possible and allowed her mind to bob in gradually like a twig on the waves. The first impression she caught was one of worry, a deep concern for the girl's situation that was nauseating in its intensity. From that thick blanket of emotion, Geh-meer tried to detach strands, one at a time, so as to isolate and read them: Jah-eed's strongest emotional thread was one of worry for her family, a young boy who lay sick somewhere; she also picked up concern for Kreh-ursh. Though having known each other barely a couple of days, the two had already formed a strong bond. Feeling a flame of jealousy lick up, Geh-meer quelled it fiercely.

Underneath these emotions were buried other threads of awareness, one of which left Geh-meer reeling. It was bound with awareness of the jewel fish, which the stranger had communicated back in Kreh-ursh's hut. Did this myth exist in her culture, as well? It was possible. Knowing nothing of the stranger's world, she thought she must ask Kreh-ursh, before remembering he was lying burned and near death — she couldn't ask him anything.

Within the stranger's thoughts was one more incredible presence, a memory flitting erratically through her awareness. Geh-meer could not fathom where Jah-eed had come by it, though the laugh with its veneer of scorn was unmistakable. Only he could have planted the phrase in Jah-eed's mind that told her about the jewel fish. Yet how could she ever have met him? Kaar-oh was dead.

II.
NIGHT TOWERS

Miguel pushed the small dinghy off the beach and jumped in. Grabbing up the oars, he leaned his back into the effort to cross the lines of huge breakers that rolled continually onto the beach. Each time he crested a wave it was as if the tiny dinghy was about to take off and fly to the moon. Then it would come crashing down into the trough of the next one. Despite a quarter moon flitting intermittently between scudding clouds, he could barely see a thing. When he chanced a look over his shoulder, the approaching waves were clear from their phosphorescence, but everything else appeared as a solid curtain of black.

Finally, well off from the beach, he risked starting the engine. If anybody heard or saw his dinghy now, they would assume he was just a fisherman heading out for a night catch. That would be his ploy to get close to the towers, as well. How he would dock there and avoid the guards, he still had no idea, but he would think of something between now and then.

Since he couldn't see them, the lighthouse was the

only sign that told him he was passing Mauri Cove's headlands. The waves took on a fresh feel, becoming high and deep ocean rollers. His boat slid down one watery slope and struggled up the next like a tired explorer trekking over snowy mountainsides. In the distance, his destination, the lights of the research station, glowed like a triple beacon in the dark.

Patrick had rung him that afternoon, and Miguel was relieved that he didn't have to lie about Jade's whereabouts when he told Patrick he had not found her. He said nothing about the talisman he had found, though, or the strange gourd that now hung from his belt, filled with orange soda.

"Where can you have got to?"

He said it aloud without thinking, surprising himself. Not that there was anyone to hear him out here. But wasn't that the first sign of going mad? He laughed at himself.

Hee hee hee ...

That was strange—as if an answering chuckle echoed his own, floating in from the ocean, or even from somewhere inside his head. Imaginings. It seemed to be taking forever to cross this expanse of dark sea. Few stars shone above despite the patchy moon. Ahead, the research station glowed like a grove of Christmas trees in the night, delineated by lights of green, red, and gold.

Miguel checked the wind. It was a strong and constant north-northeast, blowing off the sea. If he approached from the south, he might get in closer without anyone hearing the noise of his outboard, though the final stretch, rowing against the wind, was sure to be tough.

Miguel always enjoyed being out on the ocean. Before his father had been posted away, they used to come out on the water at night to fish. It was both exciting and peaceful to be out in the dead of night, beyond sight of land, waiting for the fish to bite. Yet for almost two years his dad had been working back in Bogotá. Miguel had once taken Jade out night fishing, but she had gotten bored within an hour, wanting to head in to try surfing in the dark instead.

As he neared the towers, Miguel decided not to turn off the outboard, because, instead of being shut down after the laboratory explosion, the towers were a site of frenzied activity. Powerful spotlights lit the wide expanse of water they enclosed. In their glare, he could see two small freighters maneuvering in the space between. Commands and complex strings of numbers were being broadcast over a loudspeaker system—Miguel was unsure whether from the ships or the towers—but the words were whipped away almost immediately on the sea wind. Another roaring also drowned out the speakers, mystifying him until he saw a cargo helicopter lift off one of the ships, fly up, and hover over the southern tower before gently set-tling onto its flat platform, snuggling close to the tall spire. Another helicopter lifted off the northernmost tower and headed for the other freighter: some sort of loading operation, Miguel guessed.

With so much noise and activity, his outboard was sure to go unheard, so he headed east, swinging in a wide berth to approach the most seaward tower from that side—which was also the least brightly lit. Guards still patrolled the dock, but their attention remained fixed on the helicopter operations instead of the sea. As he neared the tower's base—once again shocked by its size—he spied a flimsy maintenance gantry that encircled the concrete foundation. Just a catwalk and a single railing, it was mounted barely a yard above the highest wave crests. Yet the swell of three or four yards' difference between trough and peak made it treacherous to dock his dinghy against it. The same was true of the dock. Only a large vessel would be stable enough to pull alongside. A small boat would risk colliding with the dock and capsizing, and Miguel knew from Jade's adventure that the currents were too swift for him to swim back to Mauri Cove.

He sat rocking on the ocean a few yards from the tower's base. Jade and the strange boy couldn't have gotten onto this tower. But Miguel's curiosity was piqued, and he was getting a strange hunch that somehow she had indeed come this way. The question was how to get on board.

12.
A SCRAP OF HOPE

After Kenz-oh's story, Jade had opened her eyes to find Geh-meer studying her and accepted that the girl was reading her thoughts the way Kreh-ursh had. She didn't know why she couldn't communicate as she had before. Maybe she needed to be attuned with this girl in some fashion? But she had no idea how to go about that. With Kreh-ursh it had seemed to happen naturally, but they had also had a real need to talk.

Wasn't this the same? Kyle lay dying back wherever their world had remained, through that whirlpool thing, which had now vanished, and she didn't have the faintest idea how to summon it back, let alone any chance of journeying through it to save him. Her heart constricted as she thought of the horrible cold of the passage. It made her sick to her gut, but even though she rebelled at the idea with every atom in her being, she would risk it again for Kyle's sake. Wasn't that a need?

At first she had not understood why Geh-meer had dragged her off to listen to the story in the village square. When they sat down and the old man began to speak, his monologue was a stream of sounds that passed over her, as incomprehensible as a gurgling brook. Then, gradually, the narrative seeped into her awareness. It was as if she began to understand on a level other than that of words. This was different from the way that Kreh-ursh had spoken to her. It seemed deeper, somehow more connected to her most intimate self. And she had followed along, the way you listen to a piece of ambient music and come away with a story that is individual to you.

The legend—or myth—of the jewel fish had been impressive. By closing her eyes and allowing the flow of images into her mind, she had savored the narrative. They were not clear pictures, rather colors and sensations, but she got a sense of the tale and associations that arose within her. Something about the story had suggested that it might be vital to saving Kyle, if she could only listen carefully enough. What could it be? The Kawg-zjhur was mythical. It didn't really exist, did it?

On another level, she had been attuned to the village children's rapt silence. Yet late in the story, she had found herself drifting off and was taken over by a strange sort of daydream. In it, she had been diving down in the deep green ocean—she had had a similar dream back in her own world. She remembered lying on the beach of Mauri Cove as if it were another world. Yet here she felt as if she were swimming through transparent plastic that was solid yet liquid at the same time. It seemed to have a sulfuric or metallic taste.

Deep down she dove, noting that her limbs had grown fins, and she was able to ripple through the water with as much speed as a dolphin. At the moment she became aware of the jewel fish, she realized she had been playing with it for some time already. Its sad eye as it rolled past her seemed as knowing and mournful as a whale's. As large as one, too, yet she could have sworn that the fish measured barely a yard in length.

The fish required something of her, but she was not prepared to give it up. Saving Kyle demanded it of her, but she knew she could not do it. Tears streamed down her cheeks. She did not want her brother to die, but neither did she want to perish. It was too much to ask of her.

She opened her eyes and found herself staring at Geh-meer, who was obviously trying to read everything in her mind. She shook herself out of the trance that seemed to enwrap her, but was immediately thrown by a psychic shout in her head, far stronger than anything she had felt from Kreh-ursh. Geh-meer was staring at her, eyes wide. Her question was a single word:

"Kaar-oh?"

Jade heard the echo of that sinister laugh that had plagued her for days and knew there was a connection. She had no idea what.

Once Kenz-oh had finished his story, the village children had dispersed, so just the old man and the two girls remained under the tree. The old man had eased back until he was reclining against one of the large roots. He continued observing the two girls and seemed to be talking telepathically to Geh-meer, since their eyes occasionally flicked toward each other.

Finally, he mumbled something aloud. Geh-meer nodded and stood up. She went up and kissed the old man, then turned to Jade, indicating that they should leave. Jade also stood up. She approached the storyteller, not knowing what to say or do but wanting to thank the old man for his tale. He beckoned her closer. Quite naturally, she found herself kneeling before him. He placed a calloused hand on her forehead. Then it was as if a sigh coursed through her body, and she felt a lot of her anguish drain away. Nothing took away her need to help Kreh-ursh and her brother, but the feeling was no longer as desperate as before. She felt calmer and ready to act from a point of strength, not one of panic.

After a moment, she got up and thanked the man in her own language. Then she turned and followed Geh-meer from the gathering place. She had a lot to think about.

Down at the beach once more, Jade watched Geh-meer, alert for some sign as to what they would do next, the other girl being her only guide without Kreh-ursh. Yet the older girl stood silent, surveying the horizon. En route to the shore, Geh-meer had stopped at her hut, filled a satchel with food, grabbed herself a blanket and one for Jade. Jade grabbed her rucksack, then stood awkwardly as Geh-meer said good-bye to her brothers. It was clear they were going on a journey.

Now Jade had her blanket tied diagonally over her shoulder the way Kreh-ursh used to carry his and, strapped to her belt, a flask of the same liquid Kreh-ursh had let her taste.

While Geh-meer remained staring out to sea, Jade wandered along the shore. They were obviously waiting for something, perhaps a canoe to take them somewhere. She came across a charred circle of beach, the remains of a fire. Several yards beyond, she found another. Then another, six in all. At the far end of the beach, a lone pile of driftwood was stacked up like a bonfire waiting to be lit. She turned back to find Geh-meer observing her. Jade gestured toward the pile of wood.

"Eh-teh-kree-uu-Kreh-ursh," responded Geh-meer.

Jade nodded like she understood, though all she caught was Kreh-ursh's name. Jade wanted to ask Geh-meer about the pile, but Geh-meer had turned back to the ocean.

Jade returned and squatted down beside Geh-meer. Squinting in the same direction, she saw a tiny black dot in the sky. As they watched, it grew slowly larger. At first she thought it must be a bird and couldn't fathom Geh-meer's keen interest. But as it got closer she saw that it bore an irregular lump that didn't seem to form part of its streamlined body. Could it be a carrier pigeon of some sort, with a message? They waited in silence. Then she distinctly saw the lump move—it was alive. She gasped, thinking it was some kind of animal, even as she realized that she had the scale all wrong: It wasn't an animal at all, but a person—a rider! The bird was huge. A second later she realized it wasn't even a bird, but a huge pterodactyl or flying lizard. And it was coming straight for them.

13.
BREAKING AND ENTERING

Miguel hoped that the guards would not look across to where he was crouching on the dock behind several stacked pallets. A large industrial elevator shaft rose beside him, and they were posted on either side of its doors. As bored as they looked—more interested in the helicopters crisscrossing the floodlit sky from tower to freighter than in guarding the elevator—the machine pistol each wore slung from a shoulder spoke of a lightning inclination for changing their mind.

¡Madre purísima! he thought to himself.

Sitting in the dinghy, he had hesitated when he had seen this operation, guns and all, but suspecting that Jade might have come this way, he had to act. Of course, having his arm in a cast didn't make him feel like an absolute Superman, but he had been wearing it for a few weeks now and had relearned a certain amount of movement. To make sure he was as agile as possible, he unstrapped the carved gourd from his belt and stowed it securely under the forward bulkhead. If the dinghy didn't get swamped in his efforts to get aboard, it might survive.

As far as he could see, gaining access simply meant mooring his dinghy to this tower in high seas and clambering one-armed onto the deck, without the guards seeing. No problem: People did this in the movies all the time.

Still watching the tower, he let his dinghy drift back out into the night. He had almost decided to cut and run when a lucky event occurred: A small launch appeared from the direction of the mainland. He pulled his dinghy even farther out of the floodlit triangle of ocean illuminated by the towers. The launch was familiar. He had seen it motoring up and down the Mauri River, a small yet powerful craft.

He also recognized its occupants. It was the gang responsible for putting his arm in a cast. Screwdriver was driving. He was a skinny, bitter-looking youth who had earned his nickname for his skill with his favorite weapon: a steel screwdriver whose blade he had honed to deadly sharpness. Sitting next to him was the Head, a thick-shouldered lumbering young man, not renowned for his intellectual prowess, but whose unswerving loyalty to Rena made him her staunchest cohort. Rena herself stood between the other two, grasping the launch's windscreen cowling. This was the trio who, less than a month ago, had driven Miguel off the road while he was riding his bike, resulting in the broken arm he now nursed.

Seeing Rena's appearance—the results of Jade's latest adventure—he felt the warm thrill of revenge satisfied. While she had donned a fresh uniform since the morning, burns were still visible on her face, and she had a bandage wrapped around her head.

Another man sat in the rear of the launch. Scrawny, suited, and bespectacled, he nevertheless exuded an air of authority, which Miguel could see from the deferential way Rena turned to ask him a question. His face was familiar, but Miguel couldn't place it. Perhaps he had been on TV.

The launch docked as best as it was able. While the guards rushed to grab hawsers and steady each occupant as they scrambled aboard, Miguel saw his chance. Gunning his outboard, he aimed toward the rear of the dock platform.

He cut the power momentarily to await a wave that might carry him high enough alongside the dock and grasped the dinghy's painter rope in his left hand, the arm encased in plaster. When the next big wave lifted the dinghy, he gunned the outboard briefly, leapt to the front of the surging craft, and, placing his strong right arm on the dock as he came alongside, vaulted aboard.

He landed with a thud, and rolled. Not even looking to see whether the launch party or guards had seen him, he pushed himself up, switched the dinghy's painter rope into his right hand, and, with a firm tug to bring her bow around, sprinted for the walkway he had seen from the sea. The dinghy bobbed after him as he ran. His feet hit the metal gantry with a clang, loud to his ears, but he trusted that the cacophony of wind, sea, loudspeakers, and helicopters overhead would cover it. He sprinted around the gantry, stopping only when he was sure the tower's bulk hid him from view. Had he been followed? His broken arm hurt like anything. He must have bashed it in his acrobatic landing. The dinghy bobbed below on its painter, which was about five yards long, allowing enough slack for it to rise and fall on the swell without dragging it around in sight of the guards. He tied the painter to the railing as low as he could. A large wave might still swamp her, or if a guard decided to stroll around here, he might wonder what a small fishing dinghy was doing moored to this installation, but it was the best he could do.

He waited, listening for the sound of footsteps, but he could hear nothing for all the noise. Edging along the walkway, he craned his neck to see the group's whereabouts. He could hear voices but no actual words. One predominated, its deep, gravelly tones asserting authority. Sidling farther around the tower, he spied a stack of loaded pallets before him on the dock. The group had gathered on its far side. He crept toward it and was soon crouching behind the stack. A glance to his right showed him the elevator doors. When the group from the launch approached the elevator, he pressed himself into a shallow patch of shadow.

The guards had taken up positions on either side again, while the small man in the suit now stood before the doors, flanked by Rena and her cronies. Miguel held his breath, hoping that none of them would look to their right to see him crouching in the shadows. Looking up, he saw the elevator descending. He would have to find some way to get aboard that machine without them realizing. And, as the elevator descended toward the dock, he had an idea.

14.
FLIGHT

Jade wanted to look down but didn't dare. This was nothing like flying in an airplane, when you were so high the land below looked like a distant map. They weren't more than a hundred yards off the ground. She could easily imagine that hard surface below doing some serious damage if she fell. It was a good thing Kreh-ursh wasn't with them, she thought, recalling the sweat he'd broken into when they had climbed that subterranean chimney back in Jade's world.

The pterodactyl had floated down onto the beach at Rrurd. Each of its wings was the size of a spinnaker on an ocean-going yacht, and it had a huge, bouncy body like the Michelin Man. It burped a puff of flame as it alighted. Jade was petrified: This was a fire-breathing monster, a real dragon! Except that it had feathers, stiff ones, almost like leathery scales. They were metallic blue, blending to pale turquoise on its belly and bright scarlet at its neck. Its talons, as long as her forearm, could have taken off her leg at a swipe, yet its rider had jumped to earth and strode toward them.

"Hoh-ee. Jaa-chuunaw Kehl-grehnaa-jaan."

Geh-meer walked toward her.

"Hoh-ee. Geh-meer-jaan."

Jade knew this. Kreh-ursh had taught her—it was a simple introduction. She coughed and made the effort.

"Hoh-ee.... Ah, Jade-jaan."

Kehl-grehnaa was the dragon rider's name, and she was unknown to Geh-meer. Jade felt the rider's soft mind-touch flick over her and then away, before settling on Geh-meer. The two women began one of those silent conversations from which Jade felt excluded. She thought the dragon rider did look something like a pilot in a funny way—a bit like a World War I flying ace. She was stocky, around thirty-five or forty, and dressed in thick leather from her boots to a helmet that failed to trap much of her billowing auburn hair. A face mask—now pushed aside—must protect her face from the cold air above. Yet in spite of her gruff, almost aggressive demeanor, she appeared shy to Jade. On reaching them, she had stopped and half turned away, preferring to gaze out to sea rather than make eye contact.

The two women from this world finished their silent conversation, and Geh-meer turned to Jade, waving her toward the dragon. Jade snorted. She was hardly going to get any closer to that monster. In apparent agreement, the beast spouted a yard-long plume of flame.

But Jade felt Geh-meer's mind probing hers, maybe looking for fear. Tensing, she resolved not to let the other girl see any weakness. So clamping down on her thoughts, she strode forward to what she assumed was certain death.

Instead of being crisped like one of her mom's fritters, she found herself mesmerized at close range by an eye the size of her face. Its iris was like golden velvet, and within its pupil, the creature seemed to harbor knowledge stretching back thousands of years. She felt herself drowning in the depths of that wisdom, sucked in as she had been into the whirlpool that had spat her into this world. The sensation eerily echoed her earlier vision of the jewel fish.

A moment later, an elegant clawed foot stretched toward her and instead of ripping her open from belly to backside, it positioned itself to form a natural staircase up to its back. She felt Geh-meer beside her and sensed the older girl's apprehension, as well. It gave Jade courage to know that Geh-meer was nervous, too. Smiling through gritted teeth, she climbed onto the dragon's back.

Geh-meer followed, and finally Kehl-grehnaa. The older woman fussed about them like somebody's grandmother until they both had their blankets tightly wrapped around their bodies and were gripping a rope harness that was attached around the dragon's neck and forelegs. In addition, she insisted on tying them all together with a long scarlet sash that en-circled the beast's girth.

Then they were floating up, the earth dropping away below. If you forgot to be scared it was an amazing sight. The village of Rrurd lay far below next to its striped curve of beach. Its huts, each in its own small compound, were brown circles in the dirt, its beached canoes like fingers dipping into the bay. Shah, the great ocean, stretched away to the ends of the earth, bejeweled with tropical islands. Jade noticed ribbons of every rainbow hue patterning the water and wondered what they were.

The dragon's wing beats pulled them higher with powerful strokes. Had they not been securely tied on, the wind from its efforts might easily have swept them off its back. Once it had attained sufficient height, the dragon stretched those long sails out to either side and began to glide. The creaking and rustling of its movement fell into a silence that enveloped them like snowfall. It felt as if the three of them were pinioned onto the roof of the heavens, swaying immobile at that dizzying height in space. Over them, made almost invisible by the bright tropical sun, arched the same asteroid belt Jade had glimpsed in Kreh-ursh's mind-flash back in her world, which seemed like decades ago now. Then the dragon banked, and they swept around and began to fly inland.

*I*s this the first time you have flown?

Jade started. Up here in the air she had not expected speech, and the voice had sounded as if somebody were speaking right into her ear. She looked around to meet Kehl-grehnaa's gaze.

Feel that narrow gap between your knowledge of speech and your capacity for thought. Talk to me through that crevice.

Jade didn't know if she could. What crevice?

You just apply your communicative mind to that narrow channel between the physical world and the mental. It takes a certain knack, but it's an easy one to learn.

Can I?

If my dragon can speak to me in that way, you, who are substantially more intelligent, should not find it too difficult.

Yes, I can!

And she could.

Can Geh-meer...?

Yes. Though this isn't the same technique the sea nomads use, it is still the same power. Think of it as a different accent, like a new dialect you must learn to understand. Geh-meer and I talked about this and decided I should try talking to you before she joins in. And you see? We speak the same language!

Yes! This is bizarre!

They had been flying over forest-draped hills for several hours. In the marvel of this new form of transport, Jade had imagined the other two were as silent and awestruck as she was, but of course they must have been gabbing the whole time. She felt foolish and outcast even as she realized she could communicate at long last.

Can I speak to everybody here ... in this world, in this way?

This time it was Geh-meer who spoke up.

No. The sea nomads and dragon riders have perfected

this art, each in their own way, and the taagaag-ee, the horse nomads, also talk to their mounts after a limited fashion, but I don't think they can do what we do.

Jade detected a note of pride in Geh-meer's voice.

So, where are we going?

To Dragon Belly Lake. Kehl-grehnaa nodded ahead.

Is that the one with ... the fish?

Yes. The people also give it another name: the Lake of Stone.

How can a lake be made of stone?

That's what they call it.

Why?

This time it was Geh-meer who turned her head and directed the thought toward her.

It was you who pointed us toward it.

Me?

You mentioned it ... or rather have had it uppermost in your thoughts since I met you.

Jade thought wildly. She had not understood those strange words when she was drowning in the river, yet they had stuck with her, the sounds themselves, almost like a musical phrase. Not until she had her vision during the storyteller's yarn, though, had she had realized how the sounds and the image described each other.

Ee-kawg-zjher. The jewel fish?

Geh-meer nodded. Now it was her turn to ask questions.

How did you know about it?

Jade was bewildered.

I didn't. It was the voice ...

Whose voice? Kaar-oh's?

Kaar-oh? Was that the voice that had haunted her?
Who is he?

Expecting Geh-meer to describe him as some sort of evil demon, Jade was shocked to see the look of sadness that passed across her features.

He's.... The girl paused. *He was a friend ... but he died.*

That confused Jade even more.

He doesn't seem very dead to me!

Yes, I don't under—

Before she could finish, Kehl-grehnaa overrode her thought: *There it is ... the Lake of Stone.*

15.
HAGUES ON BOARD

Doctor Hagues had been angry all day. As he waited for the elevator that would take him up to the control room, he tried to remain calm. Those who kept calm won; those who panicked were consigned to history. Napoleon had said that, he believed; or, if not, he should have. If, as they said, a day was a long time in politics, in physics a minute could last for all eternity—somewhat shorter than a second and longer than a year if you got the coordinates right. He chuckled to himself as he realized how clever his new saying was. It needed work, but there would be plenty of time for that once he had become the most powerful man in the world, plenty of time for every-thing—though he remained annoyed.

Two days ago he had been on the point of realizing the dream of his lifetime, one that would have made him the most powerful man on the planet, of many planets—for who knew where it might have ended? He had appeared on television, both local and national channels, and been hailed as a hero by the mayor of this dreary backwater. The company had finally produced its first crop of fuel. And Synengine Energies, Inc. had a watertight patent on the process. More importantly, Synengine had sole access to the raw materials required to produce it. That was out of this world! (He smirked at this second witticism in as many minutes.)

All of that had been within his grasp. He had been on the cusp of turning that experimental process into a viable enterprise, and then—quite literally—it had all blown up in his face. Not actually in his face—in point of fact, in the security guard's face—but the entire laboratory had been blasted to smithereens by a couple of small-town vandals. He was furious.

Finally, the elevator came rattling down to the dock. Next time he would come by helicopter: It was faster, and he wouldn't have to tolerate these local goons ferrying him across from the landing. Still, they had their uses.

"Wait here on the docks," he rasped in his gravelly voice as he stepped into the heated elevator. "I'll be down in an hour or so."

He smiled again as, through the closing doors, he saw them turn to each other and begin swearing. There really was no cover from that harsh breeze down here, but he didn't want them hanging around upstairs. There were no tea or coffee facilities down here, either, but he was paying them good money, and he liked to see his employees earn their crust. If people wanted your money, they really should be prepared to grovel for it. One could hardly be expected to give it away for free. The elevator rose smoothly, and through its tiny window he sensed rather than saw the night sea spreading out majestically. The wide floodlit area between the three towers was a hive of activity of ships and helicopters. He loved the fact that he, one man, made all of that move-ment happen. And he could make it stop when he wanted. He could, if he wanted, squash any one of those tiny ants that he could barely discern on the cargo platforms and landing pads. He chuckled, despite his anger. There were always small pleasures to be enjoyed.

All was not lost. He had the police and most of the community tracking down the vandals, and once they were caught, their lives would not be worth living. Most important, even though the experimental plant had been destroyed, the main astro-extraction facility had not been damaged. The elevator doors opened, and he stepped out into the brightly lit control room. His workers were scurrying about, an example of perfect efficiency. It piqued him how they knew he was about to enter when there were no cameras on the dock or approach. That was a detail he would have to get sorted out; the company could expect a great deal more press and—more significantly—espionage interest, from now on.

His manager was standing sycophantically beside the elevator doors.

"Good evening, Dr. Hagues."

"Get me the op reports, and the reports on this morning's damage."

"Yes, sir!"

The underling was off and scuttling like a cocker spaniel pursued by hornets. Hagues wandered up to his desk at the back of the room, where he had a comfy leather armchair, from which he could survey every person working under him, as well as—through the wide floor-to-ceiling plate-glass windows—the fault, when it opened.

His manager approached, holding the reports.

"Give me a summary."

"Yes, sir. As you probably know, the laboratory was totally destroyed. The explosion was hot enough to melt all the reduction machines. While the K-2103 organism is obviously not flammable, we had never analyzed the waste product produced when we reduced this type of animal ..."

"More plant than animal, wouldn't you say?"

"Well, sir, we know it is sentient, whereas plants are not." He saw the look of annoyance on his employer's face and hastened to continue. "But the effluent is apparently highly flammable, even explosive, without requiring compression ..."

As his employee rabbited on, Hagues recalled his first glorious sighting of that "animal," as the underling called it. The sight had been splendorous. He had been young then—twenty-seven?—a bushy-tailed physicist dedicated to discovering the universe's every corner and making his world a better place. Then he had discovered K-2103 and realized he was onto something. It was an opportunity too good to be missed, and for over thirty years he had been working toward this moment—rather, the moment it would have been had the vandals not destroyed his dream. Delayed it, that is.

Still, some nights when he couldn't sleep, he ached to return to that idyllic world he had discovered, to swim once again in that ocean surrounded by his colorful friends, the K-2103 organisms, and the woman.... He wrenched his mind away. It was too much! He hated her, could never forgive her. But if only he could go back! He knew that was impossible though—the fear was too great.

His manager was onto the op reports.

"We had a wobble. More of a flutter, really, shortly before we planned to close it down."

"What sort of a wobble?"

"Well, we'd harvested the little creatures ..."

"Don't call them creatures! They're K-2103!"

"Yes, sir. Sorry. We'd harvested, flushed most of the effluent through, and gone to close down, but the fault wouldn't close. The more we downed power here, there seemed to be some sort of reverse electrical charge on the other side that held it open. We'd totally closed off power, but the fault remained open till shortly after the laboratory exploded this morning. Some sort of static field was stopping it from closing."

Hagues frowned. That did sound odd. He went over his calculations mentally, trying to think of any phenomena that could account for such a reverse energy charge. They needed to be able to control the fault fairly strictly if they wanted to flush that effluent through without the greenies getting wind of anything amiss. If the amount of effluent produced for every barrel of fuel was known, they would never get the political backing. One of their key selling points was that it was clean energy. Once they were established, it would be different—the tree-huggers wouldn't have a voice.

Yet now that he knew the effluent was so inflammable, explosive even, he was seeing some lucrative spin-offs: another low-grade version of fuel, warheads, liquid explosives.... Who knew what sort of creative armaments one might concoct with that slime? It seemed highly promising.

Miguel had a problem: He was trapped. His grand idea had backfired. When he saw the elevator coming down, he noticed that, being an industrial-style installation, the enclosed cabin was housed in an open shaft of steel girders that ran up the side of the tower. Creeping around the pile of crates so he was hidden from the guards and the group waiting for the elevator, he scaled them nimbly until he was lying flat on top. When the elevator touched down, he quietly rose and vaulted across the gap onto the elevator roof, banging his arm as he came down. He hoped once again that the noise of his landing had gone unnoticed among the general hubbub. *¡Dios mio!* It hurt! But he clenched his teeth and kept quiet. No one started screaming about a boy on the elevator roof. He was lucky.

He lay flat and waited. Finally, the elevator rose, its sole passenger the businessman who had arrived with Rena's gang. Miguel at least got a superb view of the entire coast: the twinkling lights of Mauri Cove and, farther up north, the city. The wind chill was horrendous, though, and he was dressed in just the light shorts and tee he'd worn most of the summer. As they approached the top deck, he lay on his back and watched the concrete ceiling coming closer, trying to calculate whether he would be crushed like a bug against it.

The elevator came to a stop, leaving a space about two yards high above. The doors opened, and its occupant got out. By light filtering up from a gap above the doors, Miguel saw that he was in a smallish box formed of the elevator roof, four concrete slab walls, and a concrete roof. The elevator's mechanism, consisting of huge wheels and drums of thick steel cable, took up most of the space. In one wall was a metal hatch, apparently for maintenance. It was the only exit he could see, except down, but it was flush with the concrete—no handle or hinge indicated how it might be opened. So he was trapped. He leaned against the hatch, trying to think.

16.
DRAGON BELLY LAKE

J ade first glimpsed the Lake of Stone as if it were the silvery back of a fish bounded by waves of purple ranges off toward the sinking sun. As the dragon flew closer, she saw it was a glassy lake, hemmed in on all sides by steep and treacherous-looking cliffs. Beyond, two majestic mountains soared above their neighbors, one slightly higher than the other. Geh-meer pointed.

Geh-urbh-geh-ot, big-brother-little-sister. That is where the jewel fish legend begins, and from where all life sprang.

The peaks resonated with gravity.

Have you ever been there?

Geh-meer shook her head.

No, but we know them well from the stories.

As they approached, the lake began to take on its own persona. Its silver glare—which from afar Jade had taken for a reflection of the setting sun—softened and withdrew into the water itself, where it took on a luminous glow. Even its sheen was misleading. Where late sunbeams struck the surface, an array of colors, from gold to purple, sparkled back, including ever changing red, green, and mauve tones. The half of the lake that lay in shadow rippled with pink, silver, and blue, while threads of green and orange seemed to flit like nervous minnows through its depths. Yet the overall impression of the vast lake was of absolute stillness. A memory arose in Jade's mind of entering an ancient cathedral on a family holiday in France. She had been enthralled, overawed, by a similar quiet that laid hold—a sacred gloom that kept at bay the bright and exhausting tourist summer outside.

As they circled above this majestic body of calm, no surface was visible on which they might land. Yet as the dragon spiraled lower, dipping under the shadow of the tallest cliffs, they spied a slim pebble beach with a narrow spit of rocks that extended out into the lake a short distance. The dragon circled down and alighted on this narrow strand.

Jade and Geh-meer tumbled down from the dragon's back, collapsing onto the scree, while Kehl-grehnaa followed more slowly. Every muscle and joint in Jade's body felt frozen solid and aching. They must have been flying for upward of five hours. In the end the blanket had done little to keep out the fierce chill of the air. Despite the encircling mountains and patches of snow clinging tenaciously to ledges on the sur-rounding cliffs, the air down here felt tropical. She rejoiced to feel solid ground underfoot after riding the dragon's soft and gaseous body, being lulled by its monotonous wing beats. She happily inhaled air, free at last from its sulfurous and sooty breath.

As tired as they were, Kehl-grehnaa decreed it would be too dangerous to camp beside the lake. Time was of the essence if they wanted to save Kreh-ursh, and evening the best hour for the task that lay ahead. But she allowed them a brief rest on the solid shore before they continued with their task.

Once she had rested somewhat, Jade stood up and went to explore the area on legs still shaky from the flight. Then she understood why they said the lake was of stone. All around them, the still surface conveyed a solid force that seemed to grip the rocky spit like a vice, as if the water were gradually grinding that narrow promontory to powder. She felt she could walk out onto the lake's surface, as if it were a marble floor. But before landing, both Geh-meer and Kehl-grehnaa had strongly warned her against this.

Whoever experiences the water goes mad—krashoh! Don't touch it, don't drink it. It is too strong for living beings.

So avoiding the lake, she moved in toward the narrow arc of pebble beach. Less than fifty yards in length, it curved in a perfect crescent, overhung by the towering cliffs. This caused a disquieting echo effect. The farther in toward the beach's center she walked, the more occasional sounds from out on the lake became magnified and pressed in upon her with resonant menace. Reaching the center of the crescent, she stood facing the lake. Sounds seemed to wash over her like huge green waves, bellowing and murmuring caresses.

Come, the voices seemed to murmur, *wade into our depths and lie down with us. Then we can recite for you the history of the world, so never in your life will you be curious about creation. Come to us! You are our natural daughter. Let us sit you on our lap, and we will plait your tresses, teaching you the timeless ways of those who need not be bothered by the problems from outside.*

A curious warbling as of high-pitched voices seemed to pierce her calm, but she shut it out. All she need do was wade into the water and lie down to find peace. The warbling was persistent. It was annoying and stopped her from hearing the beautiful promises of what her life might offer.

Then a bright flash tore across the lake like a flamethrower.

Je-id! Turn! Come back here!

Looking around, she spied two figures whom she dimly remembered. They were standing next to a huge winged beast that was shooting flames out into the center of the lake. She knew these people. Curiosity touched her, and she stumbled back toward them.

Stay with us! We will tell you the secret ...

Even as she retraced her steps along the beach, she felt the winsome voices calling her softly to her place down on the lake bed. Soon, soon she would go there, but first she must answer her curiosity for these strange creatures and their beast. She stumbled back along the beach, and as the sounds no longer trapped her in their echoing hollow, she recognized Geh-meer and Kehl-grehnaa and the dragon on which they had arrived. Her two companions came to meet her, wrapping their arms around her and reviving her with their human presence.

Be vigilant, Kehl-grehnaa warned. *This is a place of*

old things and old ways. Humans here are as moths to a candle flame.

Once she was off the beach, Geh-meer took her by both shoulders, looking deep into her eyes to make her message clear:

We have come for one thing. By taking it, we will upset the balance. This place seeks to maintain the balance as it has done throughout time. None of us can afford to let our concentration waver.

Jade felt sluggish and ignorant, as if she had just woken up.

What have we come for?

The jewel fish.

Of course. She remembered Kyle then. And Kreh-ursh.

17.
INSIDE THE ELEVATOR

Dr. Hagues' anger had dissipated somewhat. Not that he wouldn't make sure that those juvenile vandals who destroyed his laboratory were going to pay for what they had done for the rest of their miserable lives, but the damage wasn't irreversible.

The significant point he had salvaged from his underling's report was that they still had the capacity to generate or terminate the interdimensional fault whenever they chose. The laboratory, an experimental facility for processing K-2103, was gone. But then, it had had its problems. For example, the effluent pipe should have been much longer. According to his calculations, once the waste was ejected into the river, the force of nature should have carried it down and out into the ocean, where it would be sucked back into the fault, or naturally disperse, much as many an oil slick was jettisoned into the ocean nowadays. Despite the greenies' complaints, it would take decades to pollute the huge mass of water that covered most of this planet. By that time, humankind would have learned to live on the moon, Mars, or

Alpha Centauri. Greenies never gave enough credence to our unstoppable ability to invent eleventh-hour solutions to our own despicableness. Hagues smiled.

The real challenge, he felt, was how to find an adequate harvesting solution on a large-enough scale. Up until now, they had been dragging the ocean surrounding the fault with fine nets to pick up as much of the K-2103 as they could, then ferrying it to the factory by launch. But a more efficient solution had to be found. He thought that a new facility, arranged in a vast circle surrounding the fault site, might be the answer, but the expense would be pro-hibitive. So much of his vast fortune had already been spent on these three huge fault transmitters. Though the potential earnings were great, as well.

Somebody's cell phone sounded.

"Whose is that?" he roared.

As a security measure, no employee was allowed to bring any electronic device into the control room. He had had a series of lockers installed on the dock so employees could leave their personal effects below. Somebody was defying Dr. Hagues. He began to fume.

Miguel muted his phone as soon as it rang, but it had sounded earsplitting in the enclosed space. With so much concrete cladding about him, he doubted it had been noticed, though who knew? He looked at the display. It was Patrick, probably wanting a progress report on what Miguel had found since his visit to the caves that afternoon. His hackles would rise at Miguel cutting off his call instead of answering it. You didn't do that to adults, no matter how laid back and groovy they thought they were, but Miguel was hardly in a space where he could hold a leisurely chat. He needed to think about how he might get out of this cell, and hit on a plan that was a bit more ambitious than waiting till somebody pressed the Down button.

He examined the small room once again, this time paying particular attention to the side on which the elevator doors opened, which gave access to the tower. When he bent his ear to the floor, he could hear an argument going on. The man who had come up in the elevator was ranting, furious about the phone ringing. So it had been heard! A search was being carried out, in which the other people in the room were being made to empty their pockets. Among the raised voices, somebody began objecting plaintively.

Abruptly, the elevator doors a few inches below Miguel's nose slid open. He jumped back. He was in no real danger, but he realized a quick decision was need-ed. A narrow sill, just a flange of metal, encircled the wall at floor level. By pressing himself into a corner of his cell, he was able to step onto this flange, supported on a mere half inch of his sneakers. Looking around for handholds, he encountered a diagonal girder running up one wall. The calculating but sometimes insane part of his mind decided that might be enough if he could use his one good arm to brace himself, by pushing back into the corner.

Barely had he achieved this position when the floor—

or rather the elevator roof—dropped away below. He was left clinging to the walls of a box without a floor, two hundred feet above a hard iron dock, as huge drums and wheels mere feet away began to turn, and the elevator's rapid fall exposed him to the night air and harsh sea wind.

Hanging there in space, Miguel pondered wildly how he might escape this latest predicament. The sliding doors into the level below were shut fast, and the walls about him were smooth concrete. Moving downward was out of the question until the elevator returned or he learned to fly. So he hung there, trying to visualize his next move. The thought came to him that if he had known the day would turn out like this, no one in the world could have stopped him from enjoying his cornflakes that morning.

Time passed and his arm began to ache. Since the one encased in plaster wasn't up to much, he tried to think what to do. The situation might have been funny, had he not been in serious danger, even on the point of death. Looking down, he saw the elevator touch the dock and the doors open. Two security guards came out, hauling a young man dressed in a white coat. Rena, Screwdriver, and the Head were huddled in the launch against the cold, but they got out and took the man off the security guards. Bundling him roughly into the launch, they cast off and roared away toward the mainland.

Miguel's arm was trembling. He had to do something. At this rate, the only way he could save himself was if the elevator came chugging back up the tower, but he could see two glowing red embers dancing around at its base, and the elevator didn't move. The guards were using the time while out of their boss's immediate range to sneak a cigarette. How long did a cigarette take to burn? Would his shaky right arm hold out as long?

There was a similar girder to the one on which he was braced running diagonally across the wall on the level below his. If he could get down to that level, might he prise open the doors into the facility? But they might have been a million miles away. He concentrated on the girder below. If he crouched down where he was and lowered himself from his good arm.... But his muscles were already too tired—they would not obey him. Fear coursed through him as he realized only seconds remained before his death.

It was the first time in his life Miguel had felt real fear. The drop below his feet seemed to suck at him, dragging him downward. In sixty seconds or so, his arm would become too tired, and he would fall those couple of hundred feet and die when he hit the dock. Sweat now flowed from every pore in his body, blinding his vision and making his grip on the girder slippery. Couldn't those morons just finish their cigarettes and bring the elevator back up?

He considered jumping onto the big wheels that hauled the cables up to save himself. But they were too far away across the void, and greasy. Even if he managed to grab on, the moment the elevator was set in motion again, he would be ground to death. The wind whistled up into the cavity where he clung using his final ounces of strength. Just to let go … then it would all be over. For a few brief seconds as he fell, he could relax his muscles … then he would be done.

The wind blew harder now. It sighed and chuckled, seemingly like a human voice. Miguel found himself focusing on his left arm, the one set rigidly in its cast. As if obeying some force outside of himself, he curled his thumb and forefinger, balled his fist tight and then opened his palm. The rigid cast crumbled. He was shocked, but he flexed his wrist and the plaster broke there, too. Next he tried his elbow. A crunch sounded before the joint—held immobile for nearly a month — stretched and cracked, and his muscles swelled joyously. The wind never ceased to blow and chuckle disturbingly, but he was no longer concerned.

Feeling quietly confident now, he crouched down on his narrow ledge, and his left hand—its arm still encased in the vestiges of plaster—grasped the tiny ledge like a vice. Swiveling quickly, he released the girder and his fatigued right hand, obeying its partner, whipped around to grab the ledge, too, even as he felt his body drop from the position where it had balanced for so long. Now he was hanging by just his fingertips, his body suspended into the space below. His feet splayed out and began to explore. Soon his left foot came in contact with the concrete corner and lodged almost impossibly in that right angle. His right foot found a tiny purchase on the door frame. Now his right hand also sought the door frame, and his left found the diagonal girder he had spied from above.

A part of Miguel's mind stood in awe witnessing these feats he'd never known he was capable of. He knew nothing about rock climbing, but he had just levered himself down a sheer wall and was standing on a ledge a cat couldn't have balanced on. And he had the elevator doors to his right—he smelled survival. Stretching horizontally, his right arm sought the hairline crack separating the doors, and soon his fingers had worked their way in. He was easing the left-hand door toward himself as he clung to an out-cropping barely half an inch wide. Then the door was open, and his tired right arm, clamped around the door frame, hauled the rest of his body through.

Teetering on trembling legs in the busy control room, he expected all eyes to turn toward him. Scores of men and women in white coats were working in frenzied harmony at ranks of computer consoles. Yet, amazingly, nobody had even glanced toward the doors or seen him come in. He felt weirdly invisible. To the right of the doors was a rack of computer cabinets, and, making little attempt to hide his movement, he staggered to the far end, where a gap between that rack and the next provided a dark alcove of shadow, into which he thankfully squeezed. There, he slumped to the floor, so worn out and traumatized from the experience he had just gone through, he did the only thing possible in the circumstances: He fell asleep. As he slept, the fingers of his left hand, so recently captive in the plaster cast, crept up toward his neckline. Exploring under his collar, they encountered a red leather bag dangling there. With his fingers curled about the hidden shape inside, Miguel smiled to himself as he slept.

18.
THE MEANING OF MYTH

Drawn up on the spit's lee shore, placed upside down to protect it from the weather, was a canoe—as if it were waiting for them. It wasn't like Kreh-ursh's, which was fine, golden and elegant. This was made of a dark, heavy timber resembling stone. Curious symbols were carved into its gunwales, and beneath lay two paddles, fashioned of the same wood.

What do they say? Jade asked about the symbols.

Kehl-grehnaa shook her head.

The writing is too old. It is in the original speech of the land, which is lost.

Jade felt full of questions, like a toddler insistent on knowing the reasons for everything.

Why is it here?

Kehl-grehnaa looked uncomfortable and stared out over the lake.

Possibly for us. She paused. *When you come to the places close to the origins, time future and time past become relative events, like two halves of a fruit—of which we are the kernel. We, or somebody else, may have come and placed this vessel here for us, knowing that we would come, or for somebody else to use, as if that foreknowledge were of a past event.* She shrugged. *But looking at this craft, I feel it was placed here for somebody else's purpose, not ours. So we must ensure that we leave it as we found it.*

Unexpectedly, she turned to face Jade.

What happened to you, over there on the beach.... Here there are many such areas, like quicksands of time. If you are inattentive, you may slip and become trapped in the mud of time. Out on the lake are many such pools, as well. If you begin to feel such a grip, remember that they flow in a circular direction, from north to west, south to east.

Like whirlpools, thought Jade. *Counterclockwise whirlpools.*

Kehl-grehnaa nodded.

To escape them, paddle in the opposite direction, and outward, always outward, for as long ... as your will prevails.

Jade didn't answer, but the implications were clear.

It took all three of them to turn the canoe over and drag it down to the water. Despite its weight, it floated. Geh-meer and Jade got in carefully, heeding Kehl-grehnaa's further warnings not to touch the lake's surface. Barely had they lifted their paddles before the vessel began to move out toward the lake's center. Kehl-grehnaa watched them leave.

The water was so still and clear, Jade could see hundreds of yards down into its green twilit purity. Yet when she dipped in her paddle, the dense wood seemed to meld with the lake's substance, as if it were a tree growing through a fissure in a stone plateau. Raising the paddle felt like wrenching up a tree by its roots, only to replant it an arm's length ahead. Despite the physical effort, they advanced quickly across the heavy liquid plane. Smells of sulfur and other peculiar minerals drifted over its surface, pungent smells Jade didn't much like but didn't quite hate. They reminded her of when her school went on a trip to the geyser park to see boiling mud pools and jets of steaming water erupting from the earth. The whole place reeked with a similar nostril-wrinkling stench.

After a period—she didn't know how long, for time out on the lake seemed to stretch and contract like a rubber band—the canoe had reached the lake's center, and sat on flat water among the sparkling bronze-green rays of the sun's retreating light. Looking back, she saw Kehl-grehnaa and her dragon far away on the shore, shining in the sunset. She felt disorientated. She had traveled out of one dimension, through some sort of phenomenon—whether it was positive and air-borne like a tornado or negative like a sucking whirlpool — and been marooned in a tropical world. Leaving there the only other person she knew—critically ill —she had been carried by dragon-back up into mountains and down to this disquieting tarn. Her brother lay in the hospital in a distant world. Yet somehow the secret to his life lay in this lake. It felt like years since the day she had tried to save him in their distant ocean, when he had become enmired in the slick and they had been rescued, since he'd gotten sick and since Kreh-ursh had appeared in her world.

She wondered about her friends, Darren and Miguel, and what they might be doing right now. Could they have any inkling that she had been involved in the explosion at the laboratory? She hoped not. Her mother would kill her if she found out.

Geh-meer let the canoe drift, staring into the water. Occasionally, she flicked a glance at Jade. Jade was intrigued but concerned about getting caught in another of those mud puddles of time.

Are you looking for something?

Geh-meer frowned and shook her head. It seemed that she was not so much searching for anything on the plane of water as preparing herself for something, perhaps some ritual they needed to complete together. Geh-meer then looked at her. Jade returned her gaze, but it was some time before Geh-meer broke her silence.

We ... this lake ... I have never been here before ... but I know, or knew beforehand, that it exists. Yet ...

She glanced up and around at the jagged peaks, as if seeking for words that might be displayed there.

Our people recount myths ... though we know they are not literal stories. They contain vital knowledge for us. One of my favorites is how Teh-ot brought us fire. You might hear it and think it is a fanciful tale, but when I was living alone on the sacred isle, completing the task that made me one of my tribe, I remembered this myth in the cold and the rain; it told me which twigs and branches to look for to make fire. The myth saved my life.

That seemed logical to Jade. She had heard that

myths functioned in that sense. They encrypted knowledge to be passed on down the generations.

So the jewel fish ...?

Geh-meer nodded.

The jewel fish is a myth. Or you could say it is a lesson. But I don't know what it is teaching us, so I can't learn the lesson.

Now Jade understood. The words in her head—the *kawg-zjhur*—had brought them this far; it had given them the myth. But it had left them with a riddle: what to do? How should they interpret the myth of the jewel fish? Part of her felt annoyed that they hadn't talked about this before getting into this canoe and coming out here on the lake. These people seemed to rely maddeningly on instinct without ever pausing to employ logic in a situation. Now instinct had brought them here, to this dead end—and it seemed too late for logic to lead them out.

Let's think then, she suggested, *about what the jewel fish myth means.*

It is sacrifice, of course. Our people sacrifice themselves for the life code.

Sure, Jade conceded. *But does that mean we throw ourselves in the water and drown? You told me not to, remember?*

Geh-meer smiled and shook her head. So she did have a sense of humor.

There are two parts to sacrifice, she answered. *The jewel fish sacrifices herself for the humans, but she also sacrifices the dragon to save the humans. Why kill an innocent creature like the dragon that is only trying to feed itself?*

Jade felt slightly unsettled. She was used to the idea of self-sacrifice. It was what most Western movies and books were based on. The hero threw himself into the burning building to save the damsel. But Geh-meer was right. In human myth, we kill the dragon to save the damsel because the dragon is evil and holding the damsel captive. But if the dragon is innocent, just going about its carnivorous business like any old bear or lion, does it deserve to die?

The dragon dies so that humans might live, Geh-meer insisted. *But it does not choose to, unlike the jewel fish, who chooses her own death.*

But why did the jewel fish sacrifice herself for two humans of a species she had never seen before? Why did she see the dragon as evil if it was merely obeying the life code and trying to put food in its belly?

We can kill other creatures to eat, Geh-meer answered Jade's unarticulated question. *That is part of the life code, but we must maintain the balance—as this lake is trying to do.*

It spooked Jade to think that the lake might be conscious in any way, shape, or form. Yet more unsettling still was her realization that she had been thinking about the world from a biased point of view, or a different slant than these people seemed to have. The jewel fish killed the dragon because she had decided that human beings were worth saving, perhaps because they would be useful?

The jewel fish knew that humans would become the guardians of the sea. She had prescience.

Geh-meer looked thoughtful, as if she had not considered this.

The dragon was a beast, doing its duty as a beast, Jade went on. *But the jewel fish saw that humans would protect Shah.*

So she saved them because they would protect her world, Geh-meer pondered.

Exactly. She made a choice. We all make choices and live by them. So, to go on, we must choose our action — to find the jewel fish—and for what purpose.

Even if the people you loved died. It was like an army going into battle, knowing that soldiers—sons, brothers, and fathers—would perish. You had a choice, and sometimes you chose possible death for yourself, even for those you loved, to do good. To find the jewel fish—to save Kreh-ursh and save Kyle—they had to choose and be certain of what they were asking. Both Kreh-ursh and Kyle might die if they went forward, but would definitely perish if they went back. Yet somehow the jewel fish was greater than these lives, part of a larger scheme.

So we go on, affirmed Geh-meer, *with a clear purpose. To doubt will be to fail.* She paused from paddling for a moment. *That is why adults cannot cross the rift. They doubt. They have seen the consequences of failure.*

So only young people could do what they had done?

What does the jewel fish mean, though? It can save Kyle and Kreh-ursh, but what then? How does it affect everything else?

Geh-meer dove her paddle into the water.

The jewel fish myth is intimately connected with the creation of the world and the humans' role in protecting the earth. How or why we proceed after fulfilling the steps we can see will become clear in time.

She paddled for a few more strokes and then stopped and turned to Jade.

As you no doubt know, the ocean, like all water, like this lake, is alive. We must wait and see how it reacts before imposing our ideas.

They paddled on in silence for several minutes. At one point, Jade became aware of the sluggish yet inexorable grip of time she had felt on the beach and warned Geh-meer. They turned and paddled the canoe against the whirlpool's pull until they were sure they had regained open water.

So they had decided to find the jewel fish, but where was it?

Focus on the colors.

Jade started.

Did you say that?

Geh-meer shook her head. Indeed, the command seemed not to have come from Geh-meer, but as a sensation in her mind, from somewhere deep inside herself. Her stomach lurched and her head spun. She was acutely aware of the lake water sparkling around them in deep blues and greens, speckled with gold, as the last heavy rays of the sun stretched back toward them off the horizon. It felt trance-like, almost like dreaming. Images began to flow into her mind, strong and sharp. It was as if a channel had opened between herself and Geh-meer.... Yet also to another source.

She had a sudden flash and saw this entire scene—lake, mountains, the whole world—as a vast map of molecules, an infinite, fine cloth of tiny interconnected beads, of which all life formed part. Yet she and Geh-meer didn't. They were unconnected, like two scraps of fabric that fluttered above the surface of the world, not a part of it. How was that? She could feel herself sitting in this canoe. It felt hard and real under her. She felt the sun's heat on her skin. Yet it was like these things brushed her without quite touching. She couldn't explain it, or rather didn't want to. She and Gehmeer had crossed worlds. They were forever separated and apart from the matter that made up this world. That seemed logical in her case—she wasn't from this world. But Geh-meer? Geh-meer was from here. What would it mean if she no longer formed a real part of it? That meant the same for Jade. Even if she did manage to return to her world, would she no longer belong there? Her atoms and molecules had been transplanted to another dimension. How would they—could they—re-meld into her own world once she returned? Or was she destined to be forever an outsider, even in her home dimension?

That was when she realized clearly what the jewel fish was, and what she hoped it might do.

19.
MIGUEL INVESTIGATES

What eventually penetrated Miguel's exhaustion was the excruciating pain in his arm. Looking down, he saw that his cast was broken and cracked, useless at offering any support for his broken bones. His entire arm throbbed, and he tried to remember whether he had knocked the cast or caught it on something, but he had no memory of.... The last thing he recalled was balancing in the ele-vator shaft, two hundred feet above the dock and the ocean.

Looking around him, he saw that he was in an alcove formed of metal cabinets that arose on both sides. Ahead was a brightly lit space filled with computer consoles and larger display screens. Technicians were earnestly tapping in commands, or conferring together, holding long rolls of computer print-out paper in their hands. Beyond the human activity, a stark wall of plate glass revealed the night like a sparkling sheet of black obsidian.

Miguel was leaning against the back wall, his knees

drawn up, and his arms clasped around them. Apart from his arm, his entire body ached. Questions whirled around his brain: Where was he, and how had he got here? What should he do now? Was Jade on board? A sudden fear gripped him: Maybe she had sneaked in here to do the same thing she had done to the laboratory—blow it up. In that case, not knowing Miguel was on board, she would proceed with her plan and blow him to bits along with everyone else.

But he knew Jade wouldn't do that. Despite Rena getting burned, nobody had been killed in the laboratory explosion. Like her mother, Jade believed passionately in saving the environment, but also that a person's life was more important than any cause. Miguel knew she wouldn't put any lives at risk.

Getting to his knees, he crawled to the front of the recess, his muscles and bones complaining with every movement. Despite the destruction of his cast, he found he could stretch his left arm out carefully and place a small amount of weight on it.

The control room was awash with frenzied action. Most of the activity seemed to be taking place across the room around one particular group of consoles. Then someone spoke just to his right, so close he could hear the rasping of the man's breath when he inhaled and a sort of pop of saliva as he was about to speak. Miguel recognized the voice, like a car's tires crunching over gravel.

"How long has it been there?"

"Our patrols normally go by every hour, sir, but with the destruction of the laboratory, all our schedules were thrown off. The last time we checked that gantry was seven this morning. It wasn't moored there then."

"So that dinghy with an outboard must be the craft the security guard mentioned. It's hardly a high-powered motor launch."

"And sir, we found this."

Miguel heard a gasp and risked stretching his head beyond the shadow of the row of cabinets. Dr. Hagues was standing with his back to the recess, and a security guard was facing him, holding out the gourd that Miguel had found in the cave. So it was his dinghy they had found. He withdrew quietly into the recess. He had no other way of getting off this station.

"So we know she and her friend are on board," Hagues continued. "But where can they be hiding? And what's their plan? Implement A5 maximum alert. The entire installation is to be searched. Nobody is to pass any security point without full digital and visual ID. I'll get this little vandal and make her pay for her crime. And I'll hold on to this."

"Yes, sir!"

D r. Hagues leaned back in his armchair and caressed the gourd. He had been astounded when he saw the guard with it. His heart had begun to thump, and he could barely kept his voice steady until the underling was out of his presence, so that he could examine it more closely.

Now he could trace the gently flowing lines carved into the vessel's surface. They entwined in such delightful patterns, like the fanciful patterns created by ripples at sea. Yet they flowed together to form fish, birds, and other, imaginary, shapes. The craftsmanship was formidable. It had to be from that world. It resembled nothing that could be found on this earth.

He grimaced. This was proof. If the people from that world were crossing over into his own, what would that mean for himself and his enterprise? Would those strangers be able to offer governments here a more competitive price on K-2103? It might jeopardize his entire operation. In a flash, Hagues saw his precious dream withering away after so many years of hard graft. There was nothing for it: If those people were starting to venture out, to take their wares to the highest bidder, he would have to act to forestall any attempt on their part to traverse the fault.

Turning over the exquisite artifact in his hands, he gazed out at the black ocean, remembering another azure sea dotted with atolls and volcanic islands, each surrounded by its coral reef. His first vision of that watery world had been like finding paradise. Was she still alive? Time operated differently there—didn't float along with our world in parallel, like a placid carthorse plodding beside its harness mate, but looped and buckled, twisting away from the comprehension of our earthly reason. She might be wizened, stooped, or even dead—or maybe barely a day had passed. Would her body be as firm and young, as exhilarating as it had felt when they first embraced? Not a day passed that he didn't think of her, but nowadays his thoughts were mainly bitter. He could no longer think of her with love. She might have taken the plunge, come back with him, and together they would have forged an enterprise so powerful, they would have been king and queen of the universe—universes, even. Now that was all in the past. What remained for the future—well, they would have to see.

Miguel lay back and tried to work out what to do. His arm was throbbing mercilessly. The gravelly voiced man and his cronies thought that the boat Miguel had come aboard on was the one Jade and her friend had used. They took the gourd as proof, which, of course, Miguel knew was wrong. But was Jade here? If so, where? He needed to go and look for her, rather than hiding in this little cubby.

This was more easily said than done. From his small recess, he could see the elevator doors to his left, though he still had no memory of how he had gotten here from there. Gazing around the control room, he could see no other entrance, just the curving windows that gave out onto the night sea. If other entrances existed, they must be set into the same curving wall he was leaning against, hidden therefore by the tower's curvature. He debated which way to go. Left went past the elevator doors; right, past the gravelly voiced man.

To go either way he would have to crawl and hope nobody spotted him. It was a slim chance, but they hadn't seen him crawl in here, had they?

He chose left. Poking his head out for a recce, he saw his path lay in plain view of those working at consoles. Most of the workers were concentrated on their screens or looking out at the weather, but if anybody should glance up, they would see him immediately.

Softly and steadily, he thought. Any sudden movement would cause people to glance his way, but gradual progress might go unnoticed. That was the plan. He made sure his breathing was steady and had almost decided to move forward, when a yell stopped him.

"Sir!"

It came from one of the consoles off to his right.

"What?"

He heard the creak of leather as somebody nearby got up from a chair or sofa. Unsure whether to wait another ten seconds, he decided it was now or never. He crept out into the space and crawled as smoothly as he could to the left, hoping that beyond the elevator doors he would find an exit that might lead him to Jade.

20.
FISHING

Jade looked down into the water, wondering why Geh-meer was not the one to perform this task. Geh-meer had described her seeing skills while they were riding dragonback, which explained how she had been there in the water to rescue Jade and Kreh-ursh. So she would seem to be more suitable.

No, it must be you.

Why me?

Yet she already knew the answer. If she was right about the jewel fish, she was the one with the need. Not that Geh-meer would not give everything she had for Kreh-ursh, but she also owed her people the benefit of her skills and was dedicated heart and soul to their good—to what she called the life code—for her entire lifetime. Jade felt that she herself had no such restriction, though it would have embarrassed her to talk about the matter. It made her feel as if her own life were less useful, somehow.

Yet still she dared not act—even though she knew Geh-meer would guide her, as would Kyle. Kyle had popped into her mind unbidden, though with the thought, she knew it was true. Geh-meer and Kyle were like two channels that let her see clearly. It was the first time she had thought of her brother that way. Was this the effect of the Lake of Stone? It seemed to press into her mind and prise up new thoughts like some willful current dislodging age-old flotsam from the lakebed sludge. A mental vision arose, like a feeling, of something pushing in against her mind.

Colors.... See through the water's colors.

This was not Geh-meer but the disembodied voice again. The lake? Colors? What were the water's colors? Blue. Everybody knew that water was blue.

Look ... deep ... at the colors.

Where was the voice coming from? Why was it so familiar? Yet Jade found herself staring down obediently, even as she still resisted the idea. Blue. Water had always been blue—since forever.

Look at the colors.

The voice was insistent. She knew it wasn't the voice of that gap-toothed boy who had saved her from drowning. Nor did it sound like Geh-meer's. It didn't even communicate in words, rather as sensations, or a meaning conveyed without form. So, okay, then, to get technical, the lake water didn't appear quite blue. It looked more greenish or translucent. What color did a prism have? The green seemed to be mixed with gray, plus a touch of blue, of course. Yes, it was sort of a greenish gray-blue—with those reflections on the surface shining silver and gold ... and also another metallic sheen that was neither, similar to white gold.

Then her mind opened up further to the whole play of colors, sinking into the silent language of atoms.... Down at the most basic level of the water's fabric, molecules bounced back light rays to create different colors. She still felt quite separate, but it was as if she could listen, truly hear the structure of this new universe ... a silent music. Sensing Geh-meer's presence around her, she felt as if the other girl had attuned her to the right frequency.... She lost her concentration for a moment, before refocusing.

Water was transparent. It didn't have a color. It only looked blue ... green, or gray ... whatever you wanted.... The silver appeared from the reflection of light—all colors were like that.

Listen to the colors.

She almost recognized the voice, but it remained just beyond her identification. So she looked harder at the depths below the canoe. The water appeared blue, gray, and green within the canoe's shadow, but she began to note even more subtle tones like mauve and lilac as she stared harder. Lurking just beneath the reflections was a pallid ultramarine of the sort you see at dawn. But the shadowed sides of certain ripples revealed a deeper, richer blue—the shade of a cloudless sky in late afternoon, just before evening folded into sunset. An almost invisible indigo, a shade you might glimpse at twilight, shimmered farther down. Far beneath were purples, lavenders, and midnight blues that were almost black. Gold winked into silver and a pale pink, counterpointing a rich grass green in the body of the water. She saw yellow as bright as a candle's flame, and then the blazing orange of a desert sunset. There were colors in the water! From browns like freshly turned earth or the shiny chocolate of a beetle's back to hot sparkles inside the cooler tones, all of these colors whirled through her like a kaleidoscope.

See through.... Look beyond.

She relaxed, and saw what a few minutes earlier, she had been blind to. She felt scared, but looking deeper into the layers of changing hue, sought some essence that escaped her beneath the surface, below the fabric of the immediately visible world.

There was a twinkle, a flash, far below. She gasped. She had never seen anything so beautiful, so strange and yet familiar. An instant feeling of recognition shook her. It felt as if she were experiencing an unknown hidden part of her being, an alter ego who was her double, separate yet magically a part of her—like some previously unsuspected twin who had been wrenched away at birth and with whom she was now reunited. This process was like remembering, recalling a forgotten dream vision floating in the water an arm's length below the canoe. She was look-ing down at the jewel fish.

It was a fish, but so elegant and agile! Its body writhed, as supple as an eel's, and it turned in the water like an acrobat. Fluttering fins trailed behind like long lace scarves. Its many colors were astound-ing: green-gold patterns that pebbled its back like jade of myriad depths; crests like ruby encrustations that arched along its spine; its scales glowed orange like amber in sunlight; while the tiger-eye yellow and black obsidian of its side markings contrasted with the blue of flashing sapphires and dark crystals. Every color she had sensed in the lake rippled along its body for an instant, or in a single spot. Yet the feeling that captivated her most strongly was this sense of belonging, the knowledge that this unworldly aquatic creature was—had always been—a part of her. She had just now awoken to what would from this point onward become her most treasured knowledge.

She reached down, but Geh-meer's hand on her arm stopped her from touching the water.

Ask.

She was supposed to ask ... Her mind latched on to Kyle, and she knew what her question was. The fish spun around and floated toward the surface. A multicolored eye observed her. She felt herself drowning in that iris, as if all the knowledge she had ever known were being sucked out. The fish seemed to be interrogating her, reading her thoughts. Was it judging? She tried to remain calm and clear her mind, concentrating on her brother and his need. At first she pictured him as she had last seen him, grumpily tossing and turning in his bed, wracked by the fever the poison had caused. Then an image billowed up. She saw him lying still, deathlike but for the shallowest breathing. She knew he was near death. She looked down into the fish's eye, attempting to form a question: Could ... it ... cure him? A wave of intense sadness washed up over her out of the water.

She hated to do what must come next ... though she

knew nothing was real.... These perceptions were just a reflection of whatever beliefs Geh-meer was channeling from her world.... The jewel fish didn't exist.... Yet even so, a sacrifice was demanded.

Geh-meer pressed something into her palm. Breaking eye contact with the animal below, she looked. Her hand held a coil of homemade twine attached to the carved bone of a barbed fishhook. She had to catch it.... Looking down, she understood.... This creature was willing to let itself be caught ... killed.... A life for a life.... The life code allowed you to take life to survive. She could catch this fish to save her brother. Though the fish was not real, it would still die.

The next few minutes passed as a blur in her mind. She was aware of lowering the hook into the water and the fish twining itself around the line in a kind of dance. It wasn't a violent act but rather sensual—a dance unto death.

The next moment of which she was aware was the fish gasping out its life on the floor of the canoe. As it drowned in the air, its one visible eye began losing colors by the second, clouding over and turning gray. Its life was slipping away. Then it was dead, its body still.

In the dusk, the colors around them faded. The miracle she had just witnessed became nothing more than a fish—a yellow-brown fish dusted with indistinct speckles. Geh-meer produced a knife, sliced from under the gills, past the rust-colored fins, and down its long belly to the tail. An opulence of pinkish gray innards spilled out. Her fingers rummaged among them, messily pulling flesh from the skeleton.

To Jade, it looked barbaric—how could she mutilate such a beautiful creature, one that felt like it was so much a part of Jade's being? Yet now the fish lay there, nothing more than a pile of neat fillets and a mess of skeleton and guts. Geh-meer's fingers kept hunting. Finally, she grunted and pulled her hand free. Lying on her palm, still slimy with fish guts and blood, was a small round stone that glowed pale in the twilight. Jade picked it up. Similar to a pearl, it shone almost like gold, though of a paler hue than any gold she had ever seen.

What is it?

The other girl just shrugged. She bent to gut and clean the jewel fish as if this were a normal catch she had caught on any day of the week.

21.
SEEKING THE TRUTH

Miguel's progress across the floor of the control room seemed to stretch eternally, a never-ending four-legged moonwalk. At any moment he expected to hear a yell and have everybody in the room running at him. Yet some sort of a crisis seemed to be in motion. The workers were looking worried and remained bending over their screens, only briefly conferring with each other in nervous tones. Possibly the last thing they expected to see was an unknown youth crawling across the floor of this high-security facility. So they didn't see him. At least, that was what he hoped.

Inch by careful inch, he approached the elevator doors. Beyond, he could now see two other openings, of which at least the nearest looked like a door. He resolved to take it, not wanting to push his luck by crawling around here in the open any longer than he needed. It required all his strength of mind not to break into a scurry as he neared the doorway. But he was realizing that the key to invisibility is not a magic cloak but simply spellbinding calm. In his mind he visualized a lynx he had once seen on a nature program, and the way it had crept, in full view of its prey, with infinite stealth, closer and closer, until it was within striking distance. That was how he felt, though he had nothing with which to strike if push came to shove. Finally, he was at the door. He leaned his shoulder against it and was relieved to feel it give. It opened stiffly and silently, enough so that he was able to slip through without causing a bang or making any sudden movement.

This was good. He was crouching in an empty stairwell, with a choice of stairs leading down and up. Down would be toward the dock, he imagined, but upward? Having heard the gravelly voiced man talking about a lockdown, he knew there would be guards, but to move was better than remaining seated in that confined hideaway without any decided plan. And he must find Jade before she chose to blow this place up, as well.

Cautiously, he began to climb the stairs, keeping a wary eye out for guards or other personnel. Two flights up was another landing and a door like the one he'd just come through, but contrary to what he expected, he saw no sign of guards. He approached stealthily, in case somebody were posted on the far side of the door, where they could cover both elevator and stairs. He was just about to try the door handle when he heard muffled voices and the door swung open. Flattening himself against the wall, he narrowly missed adding a broken nose to his list of injuries.

"I told you he was nuts!" spat one of two security guards who stormed through the door. "All this 'security lockdown' for some idiot kids!"

"It's just another one of his mad moments," the other predicted. "Give it twenty-four hours, and he'll have forgotten all about it."

They stamped off upstairs without a backward glance. Before the door could shut, Miguel slipped around and through the closing gap.

He stood frozen on the other side. It wasn't the space that made him pause. Though the room he found himself in was huge, occupying the tower's full width with a high ceiling overhead. A forest of large machinery occupied most of it, connected by glass pipes that traveled up, down, and every which way. Inside the pipes, a glittering, colored substance eddied and danced in a mesmerizing way. Its animated swirling seemed almost alive. But that wasn't what stopped him cold.

"¡Oh no, por el amor—!"

Having leapt up from a loose semicircle of chairs arranged close to the door he had just entered through — coffees, colas, and ashtrays spilling from laps and knees, looking as shocked as he was yet glaring with evil intent— stood Rena, flanked by Screwdriver and the Head.

So, here we have one of the vandals," Dr. Hagues chuckled as he stepped out of the elevator and came toward Miguel. "Now we should get some answers."

"No, I wasn't involved in that explosion!" Miguel spluttered. He knew he had to prove his innocence immediately if he didn't want to be blamed for a crime he hadn't committed. "I wasn't anywhere near there. I can prove it. Even the police have my alibi ..."

The gravelly voiced man just smiled at him.

"Lad, we'll save a lot of time—and discomfort on your part—if you just come clean and tell me what I want to know: Why did you target my laboratory? Who put you up to it? Whereabouts is your accomplice, the girl? It won't hurt for you to know my name: I'm Dr. Hagues. It also won't hurt for you to know that I'm not a very patient man."

"I swear to you, sir—ask the police!"

Dr. Hagues only smiled more broadly.

"We're not going to bother the police about this little matter, lad." He waved his hand vaguely toward Rena, Screwdriver, and the Head. "We have quite the resources here to deal with this."

Miguel's heart went cold in his chest. His arm began to throb, possibly at the memory of Rena's revenge. He knew quite enough about pain already from this gang of goons.

"I don't know anything, sir, I swear to you! I came out here looking for Jade because her father asked me to."

"Her father asked you to break into a high-security facility located over a mile offshore in rough seas? I find it very difficult to believe that any parent would be so irresponsible—though, knowing those hippies, I imagine anything is possible."

"It's the truth!"

"No, but don't you worry, we'll come to the truth quickly." Dr. Hagues nodded to Rena. "Okay, tie him to that chair."

"Please!"

Miguel struggled, but it was useless. The Head and Screwdriver held him in a vice-like grip while Rena bound him snugly to the chair. She smiled when he winced as the ropes pressed into his broken arm, pulling them more tightly to his chest.

"Don't inflict any visible marks," Hagues instructed. "I don't care how much pain you put him through, but make sure you leave no bruises or cuts. We don't want to leave any evidence that might come back to bite us."

He turned to Miguel, and now his smile faded as he became quite cold and serious.

"So, who, where, how, and why?" he snapped. "I want to know who else is involved apart from your tomboy friend, where she is now—along with any accomplices—how you two managed to get into the laboratory, how you knew how to destroy my facility, and why—why two kids like you would take it into your heads to destroy such a green and wonderful enterprise as my own?"

He looked at his watch before continuing.

"I'm going to set aside one hour of my time, and I want you to give me all that information in full. If, after an hour, I am still lacking the answers to any of my questions, I will have your lifeless body put back into your rowboat, towed a little farther out to sea, and sunk. And that will be the end of you." He smiled. "Okay, shall we start?"

Miguel struggled against his bonds.

"I don't know, I tell you! I wasn't there! I'm looking for Jade, too!"

Dr. Hagues sighed.

"I'm sorry, young man, that was the wrong answer." He turned to the goons. "I'm going to step outside the room for five minutes. When I return, I want him to be in a more cooperative frame of mind."

"Yes, sir," Rena smiled, and the Head snickered. Screwie just stared intently at Miguel, turning over a worn screwdriver in his hands. Miguel could see that it was sharpened to a wicked point. "We'll do our best," She added.

"No!" screamed Miguel, but Dr. Hagues had already left the room, and the door clicked shut behind him.

22.
SPARKS IN THE NIGHT

When Kehl-grehnaa lifted them up and out of the crater lake, it was almost full night. They flew just a short distance and landed next to a stream. Kehl-grehnaa's bhaanj made quick work of the job of fire lighting, and Geh-meer had jewel fish fillets skewered and roasting over the flames in no time. Jade was shocked. Here was this amazing mytho-logical creature with magical powers, one with whom they had just shared what felt like a spiritual experience, and these two women just wanted to eat it!

She turned away. She didn't want anything to do with this. Kehl-grehnaa had also withdrawn. The dragon rider knelt beside her bhaanj, rubbing some sort of ointment into its hide among the quills, and crooning to it in a low singsong voice. The dragon had its vicious beak resting over her shoulder and seemed to be lost in the physical bliss of its rider's attentions.

Jade wandered toward the stream and sat down on its bank. The water flowed fast and clear down the hillside. She wondered whether it came from the crater lake. The water had none of that mineral aroma that had assailed them on the earlier flight—perhaps it got filtered through rocks or gravel on the way down. But leaning close, she caught just a trace of that odor. Yes, it was the same slight chemical acridness. So diluted were the minerals, though, and the water so fresh and clear, that it didn't smell rotten. The smell was almost enticing. And she was parched. Could the same prohibition about touching the lake apply here? She hesitated just a moment, then lowered her hand to the water, which seemed to fizz and boil, its energy rushing up toward her. She plunged in her hand. The mountain stream was freezing and felt invigorating against her skin. Cupping her hand, she raised it to her lips and began to drink long and deeply. So thirsty was she that soon she could not stop but wanted to fill her belly to bursting with that delicious liquid ...

"Chaa!"

She jerked around. Geh-meer was standing a few yards away. Silhouetted as the Shahee was by the fire, Jade could not see her face, but she sounded angry.

That is not good! It comes from Dragon Belly Lake! The water will make you crazy!

Jade shook her head.

No, it's good. I was just having a drink!

Geh-meer marched toward Jade and tried to haul her away from the riverbank, all the while firing emphatic thoughts to emphasize her point. Jade could not see what the problem was, but she allowed herself to be led. She could taste that the water had been filtered. It wasn't the same liquid that had filled the tarn in the mountains. However, Geh-meer did not look convinced. Handing Jade her gourd, she made her rinse out her mouth, and take a long draught.

Why is the water poisonous? It's good.

Geh-meer just shook her head again and made her sit beside the fire. Kehl-grehnaa, seated close by, handed her a large jewel fish fillet fresh off the flames.

Come on, eat. It's good.

Jade had always loved fish, and her hunger made her reach out her hand. The flesh tasted fishy, but not salty. In fact, it was delicious. Whatever she was expecting, this was a far more delicate taste than anything she had ever eaten. It was like the freshest lobster but with a faint flavor of something else quite undefinable. She didn't understand: If the water the fish swam in was so bad, how could the flesh itself be good? Yet this was Geh-meer's world. She must know what she was doing.

After eating, Geh-meer and Kehl-grehnaa sat and talked in low voices together. Because they were not using mind speech, but their own language, which she didn't speak, Jade could not understand a word. Yet she didn't feel excluded. Instead, welcoming the chance for some time to herself, she grabbed her old rucksack and opened it to retrieve the leather-bound volume and plans she had taken from Dr. Hagues' office in the laboratory.

Thinking that the plans would be of the laboratory, which was now destroyed, she thought to give them just a cursory glance. But she noticed that several sheets illustrated diagrams for the triple-towered installation out in the ocean beyond Mauri Cove. Below those, a couple of pages showed sketches of circles or spheres with lines and curves intersecting them. Was this some sort of cylindrical installation, with axes or tangents traced across it? Or maybe they were planets, orbits, or other celestial spheres? Complex mathematical calculations lined both left and right margins.

She turned to the journal. Protected in leather-bound covers, it had clearly endured a rough life. Though a metal clasp on a tab of leather had once ensured the book could be locked, it had long since ceased to function, and Jade could easily slide the clasp out of its leather band without the need for a key. She slowly turned the pages, which were cramped with a minute, precise handwriting. The faded script, written in lilac ink, was barely readable in the fading light. She would have to wait until morning. Regretfully, she closed it and returned it to her rucksack before rejoining her companions.

The dragon rider and the two girls wrapped themselves in blankets against the cold, lying as close as they dared around the fire's dying embers. Sleep came quickly. The day had been long, and Jade's reality seemed to be transforming by the hour: from canoe to village to dragonback to another canoe. She couldn't imagine she would sleep, but dreams quickly claimed her.

She was climbing again down that rock chimney behind the cave in Mauri Cove, feeling the walls becoming closer, heavier, and sweatier. She squirmed along, needing to keep going, although the rocks formed a tunnel that squeezed her between them. She had to get through. Otherwise, Kyle would die!

Breathe.... She must breathe.

The rock tunnel became the twisting metal air-conditioning duct in the laboratory. Fire raged outside, with explosions of heat billowing in through every air vent. She was burning ... roasting ... but still she had to save her brother. She had to keep going.

Then she was once more down in the concrete channel below the laboratory. Lying in the canoe beside her was a mask, carved and hideous. It was the same one the evil witch had worn, the one Kreh-ursh had showed her in his vision. She knew she would have to don it in the end, but its carved features were terrifying, so she avoided looking into the canoe, where Kreh-ursh lay burned and dying.

She was trying to ignite the black slime using Rena's silver lighter—and Rena was hunting for her, stomping along the metal grates that passed overhead. But try as she might to strike a spark, the slime would not burn. She knew that once it was lit, she would be burned up, but that wasn't important. What was important was saving *Kai-al-lee* ... and Kreh-ursh's s-land. Where was the s-land? Wasn't it Rrurd? No, that was the rude land. And Rrurd was safe. It was Kreh-ursh's s-land that was in danger. But she didn't know what the s-land was. She kept asking the ghost in the water, but the boy just laughed, giggling wickedly, and said:

"It's an s-land. Don't let the s-land die, or you'll never get home ever again. That won't save your brother ... ever or ever or ever again!"

As he giggled, the fire billowed and exploded all around them....

"Save the s-land! The s-land is important!"

"Jeh-eed! Jeh-eed!"

She jerked awake. Red pain stung her legs, burning her skin. Geh-meer ripped away her blanket. Smoke stung her eyes and throat. Coughing, she rolled, trying to wake up. Geh-meer was stamping out the burning blanket. It had caught in the fire's embers while she slept. She sat on the cold ground in the chill mountain dawn, coughing her lungs out, and tried to pull herself together. Save the s-land. They had to save the s-land before anything else. And Kyle ... and Kreh-ursh ...

Time paused. She looked up at Geh-meer. The older girl frowned as she concentrated. Kehl-grehnaa looked bleary, having been awoken by Jade's cries. But she also studied Geh-meer intently. Jade saw the other girl's eyes seem to cloud, then all at once they were wide and staring. She looked panicked.

"Jjaam shur-aw ee-kaan-rrawm!!"

We must find the old woman. We have to get to Zjhuud-geh ... now!

23.
KAI-AL-LEE AWAKES

When the red mist departed, Kyle assumed it was a sign of the end. He knew he was dying, and that cloud departing must mean there wasn't much time left.

Since he had slipped from consciousness, all that he knew was what he could feel—but in a basic way, the same way a plant smiles into sunlight or rain. Thinking was for animals. Plants live to a slower heartbeat. This space where Kyle's presence hung emanated the stable warmth of sanctuary, a sort of breathing cave. He could not feel his body here, or the world about him. Everything was dark, quiet and soft, like a cocoon.

At first, all he had known was pain—just the black virus that was eating at him, hurting him. The creeping substance had invaded his lungs, crept into his stomach, and spread throughout his body, attacking his insides like spilt acid. And his body responded by shutting down, keeping him safe.

At some point in the pain, that ruddy cloud had lowered. He had almost welcomed it because it numbed the pain of dying. But even though that mist soothed his hurt, it also stole his will. Soon it had smothered him, and, while his body continued to pump away like a failing machine, the ruby fog began controlling more and more: his breathing, the blood that flowed up into his brain, the most basic functions that kept him alive. So he learned to swap relief from the pain for a loss of control, even while he still struggled for life. Deep down though, he knew one of the two would eventually kill him: black acid or red mist. But he locked whatever remained of his awareness into a safe corner of his mind, and tried to hold on.

A single respite occurred—one that later would signal the change. The hazy presence arose from around him, releasing its tight hold. He was able to follow along on the back of the mist to that far-flung riverbed in which his sister was drowning. Together they raised her—he and that ghost—infusing her with life. They pulled her up to air, to where jade-green water exploded into fire, before he was drawn back and pressed down once again into his body's red prison. None of this could he understand with his mind, but rather with the passive awareness of a simple growing thing, a plant gazing out on the world.

After a long period, change came, as it always does— the only constant in life—and he felt how the oppressive force had abandoned him and gone. He should then have floated down like a withered leaf to die. And might have. But even as his strength waned, and he felt that the black virus was winning, he became aware of ribbons of light, of color—threads that traversed existence, pierced his own being, and radiated out into the universe like humming, living tentacles. At the utmost reaches of those filigrees of sensation, he touched his sister and knew she was trying to reach him. At a deep level of resonance, far below the regular vibrations of the physical universe, he connected direct-ly with her, created a bond, and knew he must wait, continue clinging to that battered surfboard, however much he desired to slip forever into the dark.

24.
LESSONS LEARNED

The bhaanj banked, gliding down toward the island volcano. The necklace of pearly surf thrown up by the reef looked like a jagged tear in the ocean's rich blue cloth. Inside the coral reef, however, the formerly turquoise lagoon and once golden beaches were stained black by mud that clung to the shore and extended like a carpet out through the shallows. Even if the stench hadn't risen up to meet them as they circled lower, Jade knew immediately what had poisoned this beautiful island: a slick from the laboratory. For the first time since she had come here, she realized clearly why Kreh-ursh had appeared in her world. Blowing up the laboratory no longer seemed like something for which she alone was responsible. Here was physical proof of why that action had been as important to him as it was to her: The world she had come from was destroying his world.

Jade had the jewel fish pearl safe in a pouch of pale leather around her neck, which Kehl-grehnaa had fashioned for her. She could feel it close to her body, as warm as if it were alive, the distilled essence of what the jewel fish represented. Still unclear how it might help, she at least knew it was important—vital maybe for Kreh-ursh and Kyle, and possibly for both their worlds.

Yet she had been sad that they had fished the creature out of the lake. Didn't that make them as bad as Dr. Hagues or any of the big companies that were polluting their planet purely for greed? As they flew back toward the coast, she had confronted Geh-meer about this.

The jewel fish is a myth, Geh-meer had communicated. *It exists in the past and future as well as the now. So even if you could remove it from one present moment, it would continue to exist in all other moments, unchanged. The moment in which we fished it is now the past. Yet you could fly back—not ourselves, of course, because we have already lived the thread of our lives in which we caught the jewel fish, but others could fly back and fish the same creature. We have taken nothing from the lake because a myth cannot be undone by physical actions. That is why we left the canoe as we found it, because another life than ours may need it—possibly to save ourselves and the whole of creation. Had we disturbed the canoe, or left it unusable, we might have instantly ceased to exist. The balance in these places must be maintained.*

What is the jewel fish then? Jade asked, uncertain of what she was asking because the marble around her neck felt undeniably hard and real.

I cannot accurately say what it is. It is part of what holds creation together, like a ... caulking, the substance that stops a canoe from leaking.

Like a glue, thought Jade, *a glue for the universe.* But could it help Kreh-ursh? Guiltily, she realized she was thinking about Kreh-ursh and not her brother first, but that was because he was closer, she reasoned. Yet she and Geh-meer could not help either boy unless they arrived in time. They had already been gone the best part of two days, and now Geh-meer had insisted on this detour to their magic island.

Blue- and green-robed figures looked up as they circled down to land on a cleared section of beach. Jade tumbled off the dragon, falling face first into the sand, where it still shone white above the slime's reach. Solid ground! After hours and hours on that soft, balloon back, the hard beach felt like bliss. She grabbed handfuls of it, exhilarating in a delicious sense of return to a familiar place—in this case somewhere as simple as the ground. Geh-meer also seemed happy to have landed. She removed her sandals to curl her toes in the beach and luxuriate in its solidity. They grinned at each other, acknowledging a shared relief. Kehl-grehnaa gave a quick laugh.

Neither of you will make a rider, I think. You're both too much in love with earth, too afraid of fire.

I don't know that I want to, Geh-meer replied. *I'm Shahee, a sailor. My first love is for water, the ocean of Shah. My second, for a hearth, Rrurd, my harbor. I use air for fuuraw, to fill my sails. My exploration of fire goes as far as using it to cook my food. Any more knowledge than that may have to wait for another life.*

A shahiroh approached.

"Geh-meer, you've missed your father by half a tide.

He just took Kehdurn back to Rrurd to see Kreh-ursh. Though he was hoping to see you."

He spoke in words, Geh-meer knew, to avoid others overhearing. Kehl-grehnaa had already withdrawn.

"I know. We talked by heen-holdaw while we were in the air." Geh-meer looked down, forced herself to get out the words, "I'm sorry, Lehd, for disobeying you. I should have.... I was feeling ..."

"I know. Taashou made that clear. Let *me* be clear, though.... If you ever again disobey a direct request of mine the way you did ... I'll make sure you spend the rest of your Shahee life scaling fish alone on some deserted atoll!" He turned to look at the blackened beach, and his tone altered. "Taashou's gone ... Duu-feen died ... so did the last hurzjh-faadaw-oh and his monster ... from this stain, which we still don't know how to remove. Taashou went inland, up toward the volcano. She hasn't returned. Bhawl-dresh-oh is in charge now. He's around on the other beach."

He looked at the alien girl standing a few paces behind Geh-meer.

"So that's one of those responsible, is it?"

"No!" Geh-meer was insistent. "She and Kreh-ursh, together they destroyed the danger. She rescued Kreh-ursh. She's been stuck in our world since the rift closed."

Lehd looked Jade up and down.

"Well, I don't know what she'll do now. That rift isn't going to open again. It's too dangerous. She's hardly one of us, can barely mind-speak, can't sail.... Maybe we should send her to the city."

"We have to get her back, Lehd. She helped us."

"Impossible! We aren't going to try opening the rift just for some alien ... even if we could. Holding the rift open is one thing. It was a feat we managed with all our shahiroh working together. Trying to reopen it once it's closed—we don't even know that it would connect to her world again. You might as easily tip her into a sea of boiling lava or a gaseous world as connect with her own."

Lehd smiled thinly at Geh-meer and walked off. She turned and looked at Jeh-eed. She had the uncomfortable feeling the girl might have understood some of that conversation. But the alien was still staring at the destruction of the surrounding shore, looking stunned.

Mohduut-maat, the death stain.

Jeh-eed nodded, the horror she felt apparent on her face. Nearby some Shahee and other villagers were hauling a netful of slime toward the shore. Dead fish and birds formed uneven lumps on the surface. The villagers strained at the ropes while the Shahee chanted up low waves to herd the muck shoreward and stop any escaping back into the lagoon. To Geh-meer, the action seemed pointless. Where would they store it? How would they stop it leaching back into the water?

Geh-meer picked up some thoughts from the foreigner: *aat deh ees-land... eess-lahnd... s-lahnd...* She sent a questioning thought toward the girl. Jade was thinking that something in her dream had wanted her to come here, to the s-land, to this island. But what was it her dream had been telling her? Geh-meer eavesdropped on Jade's thought: If that evil spirit had been trying to tell her something, could he be trusted? But what had it been? Suddenly, the alien cried out:

"Ohf-kurs! De-ehs-laan! Hehwurz-sey-een aih-laan... Eer nuhr de weyh!" Jade pointed at Kehl-grehnaa's bhaanj: "Feh-ur."

She pointed to her burns and back at the bhaanj.

"Faa-ur!"

Geh-meer couldn't understand what Jade was trying to say and tried to use mind-speech, but Jade was already running toward Kehl-grehnaa, who was climbing onto her bhaanj.

"Kehl-grehnaa! Faa-ur!"

Kehl-grehnaa soothed her mount, which was on the point of takeoff, and waited while the girl got close. She dismounted. That seemed to be when Jade re-membered that she could communicate mentally. Geh-meer was too far away to capture their thoughts, though she saw Kehl-grehnaa coercing her bhaanj over to a pile of black slag nearby.

Everybody away from the mohduut-maat! Away from the mohduut-maat! Clear away!

It was uncharacteristic for the retiring dragon rider to be mind-screaming at everyone within her range, but it was more shocking when her dragon opened its mouth and blew a strong volley of flame over the pile of slag. There was a whoosh! Dragon and rider were flung backward and the slag was transformed into a column of fire. It flared intensely bright, burning fast. Then the flames jumped down the beach, hopping from patch to patch of the black stain.

Clear the water! Clear the beach! Away from mohduut-maat! Fast! Geh-meer screamed.

She heard other people echoing her cry, but the flames were galloping. Already the shore was bright with dancing fire, and the blaze was racing across the water. Canoes spun and paddles were dug into the water. A babble of mind chants rose as Shahee, shahiroh, and villagers struggled to put distance between themselves and the inflammable material.

From where she had been standing on the beach, Geh-meer was forced back by the heat attacking her. She ran toward the jungle. In just a few seconds, Zjhuud-geh had become ringed by fire. Through the dancing curtain of heat, she saw canoes retreating outside the reef. One Shahee screamed as he was caught by the flames, but he was dragged to safety and doused in the ocean. The fire burned on.

Under the shade of the trees, the heat felt bearable. She could see no sign of Jade. Had Kehl-grehnaa lifted her to safety, or had she escaped into the jungle, too? Geh-meer hoped she had not been caught in the fire—her, or the pearl that might save Kreh-ursh.

25.
TAKING CONTROL

Miguel could barely think. He kept willing himself toward unconsciousness to escape the pain, but his mind remained resolutely awake. Dr. Hagues had "stepped out of the room" twice already, and each time the viciousness of the attacks of Screwdriver and the Head (Rena maintaining an overseer's role) had terrified him. They were thorough but careful, using thick wads of cardboard packaging to distribute the force of their punches and leave no surface bruises. The blows still hurt. Deep inside, he could feel the crunch of ribs and wondered how many were broken.

Dr. Hagues was standing before him again.

"Well? Are you any the wiser, lad? I should tell you, your time is running out. You have twenty minutes left to tell me what I want to hear."

It hurt to breathe, and even more to speak, but Miguel tried.

"I don't know. Please ... I don't know where she is.... I wasn't there ..."

Dr. Hagues exploded.

"Stop lying, child, and tell me the truth!" he screamed.

Twenty minutes. That was a relief. Though Miguel didn't want to die, it was a relief to know the agony would last just twenty minutes more, and then it would all be over. He was floating on a cloud of red pain. Waves of oblivion seemed to lap darkly at the edge of his awareness like ripples preceding a tidal wave—a big, dark, heavy mass of water that was banking up on the fringes of his consciousness, a moving mountain that he prayed would come cascading down on top of him so as to drown his suffering once and for all. It hovered there but would not break, bringing its final release. Through his torment he heard voices—the goon gang and Dr. Hagues talking, discussing whether someone would say any more, whether it wasn't better to ditch his body and be done. Him. They were talking about him. He wished they would finish it so he could be free.

Then the tone changed. Doors slid open. Forcing his eyes open, he saw Hagues in front of the elevator, facing a blur of white coats. Something had become an emergency. Then Rena was standing before him, blocking his vision — was it so that their handiwork couldn't be seen by the scientists? The voices were claiming it was too dangerous to open the fault. It would cause a weakening of the dimensions … destroy both worlds. But Hagues was yelling, angry now, his deep voice like a wolf's growl.

"I want it open! We have a chance to harvest and process now that this installation is up to speed. Once it achieves full power, not only will we control the fault, but we can also harvest the K-2103 using the matter filters. Then we'll make a difference!"

Other voices were arguing, trying to convince their leader otherwise. The installation remained untested, they claimed. The station might control the fault, but they didn't know how the processing facilities would work. More tests were required.

Everything went hazy then, the pain was too much. He hoped Screwdriver and the Head would not lay into him again but feared they would soon remember he was there. Hagues' voice rumbled on.

"How long are we talking about?"

"Six months at least ..."

Within the red mist that Miguel inhabited, he began to hear a familiar whistling, like the sea wind. It seemed to groan and chuckle around him. Time passed and the voices faded, so he was unsure whether they had left the room or he was slipping into unconsciousness. But his left arm, the broken one, began to flex and shrug at the rope coils. Tensing the muscle and then relaxing, it loosened the bonds. His hand forced itself up until it could touch the red bag hanging at his breast. Then his elbow pressed out, but the bindings remained tight. He took a deep breath and, as he exhaled, pushed his arms outward against the ropes. It occurred to him that what he was doing should be painful, the ropes cutting into his arms. Yet he felt no pain.

He continued to flex and loosen his bonds, before managing to slide one hand around as far as the knot holding him captive. His fingers reached it and began to tug before finally the rope loosened. His other arm flexed and shrugged off the ropes holding him to the chair. Only his legs remained bound while ropes lay loosely across his upper body.

Hagues swore and stepped into the elevator, taking the white coats with him. Once he was gone, Rena and her mates relaxed. She went over to join the other two, who were slouching off to one side of the room. None of them noticed that Miguel had freed himself. But he needed a distraction, or else the moment he bolted for the door, they would be after him.

It soon came. Screwdriver stood up and put his jacket on.

"It doesn't take three of us to terrorize that little runt, I'm nipping down for a smoke," he declared.

"I'll join you," Rena said. "Head, you stay here. When we come back, we'll give you a break, too." She glanced over at Miguel. "And give the runt another going-over."

Once they had gone, the Head stood up straighter, conscious of the importance of his position as sole guard. Despite clearly trying to ignore Miguel, he was unable to avoid throwing surreptitious glances his way.

"I bet this has to be the lowest job you've had yet, isn't it," Miguel slurred. "Beating up a fourteen-year-old kid?"

The Head shrugged. "It's a job. Don't talk to me—you shouldn't."

They sat in silence for a few moments before Miguel spoke again.

"So you're on guard duty while they go down for a cigarette?"

"Shut it, will you? I said, don't speak." The Head was clearly feeling uncomfortable.

"So hit me again," Miguel sneered, hoping madly the Head wouldn't take him at his word. "I'm just saying what I see, that you do the work while they sit around.

It doesn't seem fair."

The Head seemed to give Miguel's opinion some thought.

"Go on, take a break," Miguel insisted. "Look, I'm tied up. I'm hardly going anywhere. Give yourself five minutes. If Rena and Screwie come back, I'll whistle, so you're warned."

The Head looked dubious but finally relented. "Okay, five minutes, but you try anything and I'll break both your arms."

"You can trust me," breathed Miguel. "Just don't go down onto the dock, or you'll run into them." He looked around. "Better go in there." He nodded toward a door that led off the opposite side of the room to a space that looked similar to the one they were in.

The moment the Head had disappeared in that direction, Miguel bent and untied his ankles before leaping toward the door he'd come in through. Though he felt pain, his feet pounded furiously up the steps. The red mist that enwrapped him so tightly he seemed to breathe its dense vapor cushioned him from the most excruciating agony; otherwise, he knew his body would be incapable of staggering so much as a foot. With no plan except to get as high and as far away from that torture chamber as he could, he climbed frantically toward he knew not where.

26.
THE OLD WOMAN AND THE GIRL

hehaw, the sight, generally struck with little forewarning. Yet she recognized the feeling — from that infinitesimal moment before the vision gripped her in its talons. Standing there, in the underwater gloom of the undergrowth—aware of the island around her like some panting creature—Gehmeer could sense its impending presence. But it had not yet gripped her as it normally would.

Instead, the entire land mass around her seemed to be swaying, almost pulsating with living energy. It felt as if Zjhuud-geh might had been ignited by the same fire that was razing the alien sludge beyond its beaches. The sacred island appeared to be breathing in deep shuddering pulls, drawing age-old power from the roots of the ocean floor and channeling it upward through the depths.

This force had infused even the tiniest leaf. The island itself and the life it harbored were trembling with a newly awakened prescience.

Go, it seemed to say. Find her.

Geh-meer stumbled, trying to feel the vision, or what it was asking of her. She turned and began climbing up through the jungle, heading for the summit.

A long time later—maybe a sixth of a tide cycle since she'd left the fire burning on the foreshore—Geh-meer felt she had not climbed much higher up the somber volcano's flank. She felt lost and unsure of where she should be heading. After drinking some potion from the flask at her belt, she pulled her amulet from around her neck, where she kept it protected in a soft leather bag the color of new moss. Sliding the delicate wooden shape into her hands, she squatted down and let the vision return, allowing the energy to feel its way through the wood.

Up, it said. *Toward the cone still.*

So she kept climbing.

As she ascended, her thoughts sifted through everything that had happened in the last few days. Having traversed mu-orl-rehn-baa, the whirlpool passage, without quite realizing what she was doing, she had found herself in that strange sea just before sunrise, a third of a tide cycle by canoe from the coast—maybe two thirds if you had to swim. She began swimming shoreward, creating a wave and surfing it the same way she had navigated the rift. When the sun had risen on the sea, its rays had picked out a canoe coming toward her, one she recognized as a Shahee craft. As she swam for it, she saw a strange girl in the stern, who clearly had no knowledge of handling a tiller. When Geh-meer climbed aboard, she found Kreh-ursh, burned and near death, so there had been no time to think. First she had managed to stall the hostile craft pursuing them, then bring them back through mu-orl-rehn-baa with no time to think or be scared.

While it felt like she was in the alien world for barely more than a moment, much more time had passed in Shah. It was as if time ran differently between the two dimensions, or maybe mu-orl-rehn-baa altered its flow.

The trees thinned. Above was the cone, scree and bare rock stretching unbroken to the sky. She was about to consult her amulet again when she sensed another presence. She forced her muscles to relax, pretending that she was unaware of the other's presence—whether human or animal. Then she spun around, whipping her knife from her belt as she did so.

A figure was sitting on a low boulder, half hidden by one of the last scraggly bushes of the jungle canopy. How worn, how grimy and exhausted she appeared! Her tunic was dirty and torn, her hair unkempt. Geh-meer could scarcely believe that this was the person she had respected and feared more than any other ever since she had been a girl.

Hoh-ee, Taashou, she breathed.

Hoh-ee.

The voice in her mind was a mere whisper. Geh-meer tried to console her.

I ... I'm sorry about Duu-feen. I wish I could ...

Speech seemed inadequate to communicate what she felt, her real feelings.

Thank you. I never imagined that it would be I who must finally wait here before following on. I couldn't leave.... They wouldn't let me leave!

Life is ... unpredictable, even with bhehaw.

Yes. We must get the girl back to her world. It is crucial ... for our world, too. To save the boy.... The boy is important.

Geh-meer wanted to ask which boy, but as if to underline her thoughts, Taashou said out loud:

"O-tohn-aw ee-kaanaa. Ee-kaanaa ehl-aw duuneet."

The one ... Kreh-ursh? You mean him?

No, the other one... Kai-al-lee.

One-of-far-touch? Who is that?

The sick one, in the other world. You have to reopen mu-orl-rehn-baa.

Taashou, you must come back. We need you.... Shah needs you. We cannot do this alone.

Taashou nodded, and sighed.

How much I wanted to move on! They wouldn't let me. There is still much work to be done here.

Geh-meer knew little about what pact the old woman might have made with her spirits in her time, so said nothing. She put her arm around the old woman's thin waist and helped her up. Together they began the slow descent to the beach.

27.
AN OBJECTIVE

The elevator doors opened, and Dr. Hagues reentered the control room, followed by the scientists with whom he had been arguing earlier. He went directly to his leather armchair and threw himself down in it while the white coats waited a few paces to his left.

"The boy can tell us nothing. We need to find that girl."

He began studying the displays on the screen before him.

"So these are this morning's readings, are they? What's that?" he snapped, pointing at a blip.

The older of the two men leaned in.

"Uh," he stammered. "Some sort of a body that moved through the fault ... perhaps a dolphin, or a large tuna? A manta ray?"

"Look at the density and mass readout. It couldn't be a fish."

"Well, a log, then. It must be a log that was caught in the fault's gravi-tational pull."

"I employ you for your brains, idiot, not to tell me

tall stories. Confirm for me what those density readings tell me, or you're fired."

"Yes, sir. It is a hard, inanimate object, such as a tree trunk, but moving at a faster rate than such a thing could achieve, even accounting for the fault's gravitational pull, which at that point in the vortex is extremely strong. The complicating factor is that other masses are contained within the overall display—two, possibly three—suggestive of living tissue, though thick vegetation or moss sometimes exhibits a similar—"

"At that temperature?"

No, sir, that temperature would indicate—"

"Yes?"

"Living beings, sir. Living beings perched on an object such as a trunk, or—"

"Or?"

"Or a craft or vessel of some description, sir."

"Finally. So? Conclusion?"

"Two, possibly three beings, in some form of propelled craft have traversed the fault in inverse direction, sir."

"Ten gold stars to my top scientist!" snarled Hagues. "So they escaped through the fault, meaning they've warned people there. They'll be preparing to fight. We haven't a moment to lose!"

"But, sir, we don't know that they are planning—"

"Have you been there?"

"No, sir."

"Well, I have! I know what they're like. We open the fault and flush through enough effluent to keep them occupied; meanwhile, we harvest as much as we can, then shut it back down. I won't let them deprive me of my rightful fortune."

"Yes, sir."

As Hagues stared out at the stormy night, his underlings scurried to do his bidding.

Miguel must have pounded up twenty flights of stairs before he heard Screwdriver's bloodcurdling yell from below. His escape had been discovered—now he needed to hide. Apart from the gang of goons, how many other guards did this facility employ? Two were posted on the dock. Were there more? He felt no pain in his body now, rather a feeling of euphoria, infused with the particular strength he felt from the ruddy cloud that had supported and nurtured him through his ordeal.

Without warning he came into a wide circular room that occupied virtually the tower's entire diameter. Snaking up around the circular wall was an iron staircase, and the ceiling far above consisted of a complex network of girders and industrial glass, with an octagonal reinforced center that served as a helipad. Two rotary blades projected over its edge, visible through the floodlit panes.

Looking around, Miguel tried to judge whether he would have time to climb the staircase before Rena and Co. erupted from the stairwell behind. To his left were three doors; beyond them, an industrial winch hung from the ceiling girders. First, he tried the doors. The first two were locked, but the third opened to reveal a storeroom. Trying and failing to think how these rooms might serve as a diversion, he turned back to the winch. Could it carry him up to the ceiling? Then, recalling something he had seen in the storeroom, he had an idea.

As he ran back to the storeroom, he simultaneously struggled to pull his t-shirt one-handedly over his head.

"¡Madre mia!"

He was forced to slow down and deal with his t-shirt first, before reaching the room and grabbing an empty canvas bag from a stack he had seen, and some plastic ties. Returning to the winch, he hooked the bag onto it, padding it out with a broken cardboard box from the storeroom. He arranged his t-shirt over the top, attempting to make the affair look as much like a teenager hiding in a cargo bag as he could. Next he took the control panel—of solid industrial casing with Up, Down, and Emergency Stop buttons attached to a ten-yard length of electric cable—and used a plastic tie to fix it to the winch chain just above the hook the bag hung from. Last, he took another tie and fastened it around the control board so that it sat snugly over the Up button.

He could hear feet on the stairs. After checking his handiwork, he pressed Up and pulled the plastic tie tight to hold the button down. As he stepped back, the winch slowly rose from the floor, carrying its cargo of poorly disguised boy along with its own control board. He slipped into the storeroom and pulled the door to. Through a crack he was able to see the winch hook rise, stretching the power cable up to its fullest extent. He had a tense moment as the cable became taut. He had no idea which would give first, but with an angry buzz, the winch pulled its own power cable partially from the wall. Instantly, the whole affair went dead, leaving the bag hanging with zero power ten yards above the floor.

"Now we've gotcha, runt!" Rena screeched triumphantly as Miguel silently pulled the door fully closed and found to his joy that the handle had a latch by which he could lock it from the inside. He remained absolutely still, scarcely daring to breathe as he listened to the gang's mood change from jubilation to consternation, and finally frustration as they pondered how to get the runt down from where he had hitched himself. Orders became threats and eventually rage, but the boy hanging from the hook in the center of the space remained unmoved.

Peering around his hideaway by the dim glow from a row of LEDs, Miguel realized that in addition to the stack of canvas bags, and mops and buckets, the tiny space contained fuse boxes and an electrical panel. He saw a light switch beside the door but decided against using it in case the gang saw the line of light under the door.

He was interrupted in his musings by a shriek from outside. From the commotion, he deduced that the Head had decided to reach up and pull on the hanging power cable, giving himself a nasty 380-volt shock for his troubles. He was apparently laid out on the floor while Rena and Screwdriver tried to revive him.

This gave Miguel an idea. Cautiously, he opened the plastic cover of the electrical panel to examine the labeling on the switches in the dim light. They were all lighting and power circuits.

"¡Genial! Será una capa de invisibilidad," he breathed. He flicked all the switches, and everything became pitch black.

"Geez! What's happened now?" he heard Rena snarl.

"The power's cut off. Must have been the Head grabbing that cable."

"I can't see a thing. Where's the Head?" As if in answer, the other boy groaned.

Smiling to himself, Miguel carefully unlocked the door. Quietly opening it a sliver, he checked that everything was dark outside. The trick would be to slip across without being heard—or bumping into one of the gang. As a precaution, he shucked off his trainers and tied them around his neck. Then he slipped out of the door and crawled noiselessly across the space to the far wall. Luckily, the goons were making such a racket, it was easy to give them a wide berth.

Negotiating the iron staircase was another matter. A few times he froze as the gang reacted to squeaks and once a soft clang as his foot hit a metal stair riser. But each time they assumed it was the boy hanging from the hook who had made the noise and responded by hurling a barrage of abuse upward. Finally his hands found the top of the staircase.

He went through a door and found himself in an empty control room. The lights there were working. Screens occupied one wall in front of a large control desk. After locking the door, Miguel approached it and ran his fingers over the keyboard. Some force motivated him to tap randomly, even though he had no idea what combination of keys would work the equipment. Time and again the lights on the console flashed red as he typed, and an acoustic signal beeped. Finally, his hand was still. Miguel wondered who or what could control him like this. Then his right hand lifted and smashed into the keys. He felt the pain right up his arm.

"No!"

Surprisingly, whatever force was in control seemed to pause and take stock. Miguel realized he might have only one chance.

"We need to find someone who has the knowledge."

In a split second he had become complicit with the mysterious presence, but he didn't want any more pain, could not take any more, not after the beating he had endured.

"We'll find someone," he whispered, unsure how he would keep his promise. "One of these people will know. We will make them help us."

28.
BACK TO RRURD

When Geh-meer and Taashou stepped out onto the beach, the conflagration had almost burned itself out. Those who had been cleaning the slime were congratulating Kehl-grehnaa. She, having advised them that it was the alien, not she, who had been their savior, sent a mind-call to her other riders, and was retreating, remounting her dragon. Fire … "faa-ur" in Jade's language, had des-troyed the slime. Where the mohduut-maat had burned, just dead ash remained. The other death stains that had come through mu-orl-rehn-baa, still floating on Shah, could now be hunted and burned up one by one. Bhaanj-ee and Shahee together could clean up the ocean. The atmosphere on the beach felt jubilant.

Geh-meer looked around for a comfortable spot where Taashou might rest, and finally led her to a wide, flat rock that lay in clean sand close to a rocky prom-ontory. Once she was out of the jungle, seated on the beach, and feeling the salt air on her face, Taashou seemed to revive somewhat. Perhaps she had used the walk downhill to lock her grief for her dead companion away in some private corner of her being. Though weak, she had regained her customary stern, cool composure. Yet Geh-meer could see she remained agitated. Shahee and shahiroh came hurrying up almost immediately, offering condolences, but she waved them away and requested the great canoe be prepared to travel.

Where to? Lehd asked.

First Rrurd, then Kaa-meer-geh. During their descent from the volcano, Geh-meer had told Taashou about Kreh-ursh and the journey to the Lake of Stone.

Taashou nodded. *The hurzjh-faadaw-oh should come, too.*

Jah-eed?

All three hurzjh-faadaw-oh are needed: Kreh-ursh, Geh-meer … the alien. All needed.

Next her gaze drifted over the beach until it located Jade, who, having taken shelter in the jungle during the blaze, had come out onto the beach again as it died down. Now she had a branch in her hand and was using it as a shovel, helping the Shahee to push blackened sand into a pile at one end of the beach. Geh-meer went and fetched her, and they walked together back toward Taashou. Sensing her friend's nervousness, Geh-meer flashed her a smile, trying to put the girl at ease. They came to a halt in front of the old woman. Taashou said nothing at first, merely examining Jade with those dark, stony eyes. Finally, she nodded.

She is a hurzjh-faadaw-oh, though I have no idea why she has been chosen.

She claims she was there, Geh-meer offered. *On the beach, when Kreh-ursh arrived. She's been hearing a voice … Kaar-oh's.*

Taashou frowned and turned to Jade, at which point Geh-meer realized that the shahiroh had been skillfully shielding their mind-speech from Jade, something Geh-meer would not have been capable of.

Welcome to Shah, stranger. Thank you for saving Kreh-ursh. He is a precious member of our clan.

Jade nodded warily. Though she recognized this woman from the vision Kreh-ursh had shown her, she did not really understand who she was, except that she wielded power. At the mention of Kreh-ursh, she felt concern.

We must go to Kreh-ursh … to help …

Not quite knowing what she meant, or how to say it, she loosened the pouch around her neck and produced her prize from the Lake of Stone.

Taashou was instantly alert as she leaned toward Jade's hand. She made no move to touch or pick up the pearl but scrutinized it carefully.

Yes, she nodded. *If this does not help him, we can do nothing.*

Jade sat in the bow of the great canoe, reveling in their speed through the huge ocean waves, some of which had to be five yards from trough to peak. Large as it was, the canoe still plunged into valleys and smashed through the wave crests twice as high as she was long. Each time the canoe tore through the top of a wave, a blanket of water soaked Jade. The rest of the crew seemed to eye her as if she were crazy, but Jade exalted in the surf, feeling more alive than she had at any moment since arriving in this world.

Something was happening, she could tell—a change had begun. Some subtle balance had shifted in her relationship with these people, in part to do with her suggestion of using fire to defeat the slick, but also because of the old woman's reappearance. The Shahee appeared to have regained hope, and their attitude to her had changed, as well. No longer were they treating her as a representative of the black poison that had been destroying their home; several had offered her a smile or nod as they passed her on the beach, and nobody now avoided her gaze.

Jade felt uplifted, exhilarated. She was breathless to know they would be seeing Kreh-ursh soon, much as she tried to hide her feelings from Geh-meer. And she knew that the path to the village might also lead her back to her brother—Kai-al-lee, as these people called him. The jewel fish stone formed a solid, constant weight around her neck, radiating warmth into her breastbone. In a way, it focused, calmed her. If it could help Kreh-ursh—and these people seemed to think it could—might it not truly be her brother's salvation?

Further back, Geh-meer and the old woman huddled together, sometimes mumbling in words, other times locked in mind speech. Yet Jade remained in the bows, exulting in the salt air fresh on her face.

When the Great Canoe finally left the blowing sea and glided across the quiet lagoon, it seemed to sigh in relief. Jade was cheered by the sight of Rrurd across the bay—the only place she had returned to since she'd arrived here. As they hit the beach, the Shahee sailors jumped over the side and hauled the huge vessel far up the beach. Jade scrambled out and turned to help Geh-meer with Taashou. The old woman's grip was like steel. Before Taashou let her go, she held Jade's hand for a moment, scrutinizing her shrewdly.

Why do you think you have been called?

Jade felt flustered.

Sorry? I was not …

Who called you?

Had she been called? She was confused. Knowing that the old woman could read her thoughts as if she had spoken them, Jade didn't answer. She hadn't been called, unless you could count that voice in the water, but they had already established that that was Geh-meer's dead friend, and apart from being dead, he was a child, no powerful sea caller like the old woman.

Standing there in the shadow of the Great Canoe, Jade wished she could offer the woman answers. She felt odd, as if she were carrying a weight of responsibility, but she didn't know what, or for whom.

The moment was broken by a shout from the canoe, and Geh-meer shot past them like a flash. She threw herself into the arms of a stocky older man who had been standing next to her brothers. Her father. Taashou turned and began to walk up the beach, pulling Jade after her with a vice-like grip on her wrist while resting heavily on her arm. Jade barely had time to smile and nod at Geh-meer as they passed the family group, though the other girl didn't notice.

Then they were in among the huts. By now, Taashou's spurt of strength had waned, and Jade found herself almost carrying the old woman. As she was hoping, they headed straight toward Kreh-ursh's compound. Outside stood Kreh-ursh's mother and a surly man who glared with open dislike at Taashou. He was the spitting image of Kreh-ursh but older, more solid. He was dressed, like Geh-meer and her father, in Shahee green.

"Hoh-ee, Kehdurn," the old woman muttered.

"Hoh-ee, Taashou."

Kehdurn's feeling for the shahiroh was palpable.

Then there ensued what felt to Jade like a heated — silent—conversation, one from which she was exclud-ed, before Kreh-ursh's father stood aside. Taashou then ducked into the hut, pulling Jade after her.

29.
TECHNICAL CHALLENGES

Standing alone in the control room atop the tower, Miguel spied a power switch to the right and flicked it on. Screens flickered into life, showing different areas of the installation. He was pleased with this early success, and his hand rose to his throat, where it began stroking the lovely shape hidden in its red leather pouch. He felt calm and happy, knowing he was going to help Jade and her friend.

Wait. How did he know about the friend? Well, he knew from Patrick and Officer Schreub that Jade had an accomplice. But how did he know that the accomplice was basically good, that Miguel should be helping him? He just knew—there was no need to think about it. He felt content with that answer and felt that he could act decisively if the need arose.

From the screens, he saw that each tower contained a huge coal-burning generator. Graphs showed the huge amounts of power they produced. The ships he had seen earlier were still unloading their black cargo into each tower, delivering it from their holds into giant hoppers mounted on the sides and top of the towers. Other screens showed giant furnaces, stoked by conveyor belts laden with coal.

One screen showed a series of smaller machines: bell-shaped and bolted to the floor. Glass tubes pierced them and formed interconnections with the other furnaces. Through the tubes flowed a glistening substance that seemed to sparkle and flash in innumerable colors. It reminded Miguel of something he'd seen on television earlier that day, but exactly what that was he couldn't quite recall.

He was drawn to one screen in particular. It showed the control room below, where he saw Hagues, still arguing with his scientists. They did not want to open the fault, but Hagues did because he wanted his profit, his power. Miguel suddenly knew that that was the right thing to do. The scientists were being overly cautious. Once the fault was opened, he might travel back to that ocean more beautiful than any in existence. Shah. Even the name felt like a beautiful dream. Miguel sighed. Finally to be Shahee. It was all too good. All they had to do was open the fault. Did Hagues know the combinations to do that? Or was it the scientists? Miguel watched them, straining toward the screen, determined to absorb every detail. It was up to him to learn what had to be done. Yet how to do it? He had no idea what it meant to open a fault. A cloud began to form in his mind, and he sank into a chair with relief.

In his mind, a beautiful blue sea unfolded. It was dotted with islands, some harboring volcanic cones from which the odd trail of smoke curled. Huge pterodactyl creatures planed above the water, diving occasionally to grab fish in their beak or talons. Coral reefs wreathed many islands, and a pale-pink asteroid belt stretched across the sky. It was a beautiful world.

The scene changed, and he saw a village nestled on the shores of a large cove. As the vision drew nearer, it focused on a gathering of villagers, mainly young people. Boys and girls were dressed alike, barefoot and in simple brown and green tunics, though the girls took his breath away. Beautiful, dusky, and long limbed, with shining dark hair hanging to their waist, they were dancing. Though he couldn't actually hear the music, he felt as if it were playing in his head—pipes and wind instruments over deep, insistent percussion. Watching the girls flowing with the music, Miguel knew he wanted—had to go there. To live in such a place would give his life meaning.

Then that scene vanished, replaced by one of a stormy sea with an ominous twister dominating the sky, which seemed to suck everything into its black maw. He recognized it, but was at a loss for a few moments before realizing that it was the same vicious storm that had battered Mauri Cove a few days ago. Come to think of it, that wasn't the first time he had seen a thing like that off the coast. He couldn't work out why it hadn't stuck in his memory. But whatever was controlling this vision pulled his mind back toward the whirlpool-like vortex—it was bizarre how it appeared like a tornado at first, then seemed to turn itself inside out as you looked and became a tunnel spiraling down into watery death. Beyond it, he was aware of the girls dancing, ever more frenzied, and he wanted to be with them more than anything in the world. Now he knew what he must do:

He must open the fault.

Miguel looked back at the screen. Dr. Hagues was nowhere to be seen, and the scientists in the control room appeared busy again. The doctor must have disappeared while Miguel was dreaming about the beautiful dancing and that pure blue ocean. How could he have fallen asleep at such a time? He must get back on track—there was something he had to do, find someone ... Jade, his friend ... that was who ... plus her friend ... and go somewhere, open a fault or rift.... His objective crystallized: Yes, he must open the fault to save Jade, however he was able. To do that, he must enlist the help of these scientists, for they held the knowledge he needed. Like the shahiroh, they were wise ones.

Where was Dr. Hagues? He wanted to open the fault, too, and could order it opened. But he was gone off somewhere ... Miguel didn't know where. He would have to deal with this himself, but how?

He had no real idea even what the fault was—some sort of huge crack in the sea floor that would be winched apart?

The door opened, and in walked Dr. Hagues.

"Progress report?"

A woman, one of the white coats standing at the consoles, turned toward him with a readout, but before Hagues could take it, his attention was grabbed by a low hum.

"Where's that coming from?" The noise—so low it was more of a vibration than a sound—seemed to be oscillating throughout the tower. "Whatever," Hagues snapped. "Continue with the operation."

But the hum was rising slowly in pitch, and as it went up the scale, the physical vibration became stronger, so that soon they could all feel the tower shaking.

"Display stabilizer readouts," snapped Dr. Hagues, heading for his armchair, from where he could monitor the master display screens.

The woman who had handed him the readout earlier—clearly somebody with authority—turned from her console: "The localizer beacons seem to be overheating by 13.67 per minute, sir. They are not res-ponding to the circuit-breaker protocol."

"How long till we achieve minimum breach energy?" asked Hagues.

"Six and a half minutes, sir, but by that time we will be at 88.85 of the critical heat operational ceiling. Should we abort?"

Hagues shook his head. "No, once the fault is open, the dual magnetism between dimensions will take over as the primary drive factor, meaning we can throttle back power in under seven minutes. That's plenty of time."

"We've never trialed this, sir." The woman looked stressed. "Permission to stall the power curve until we can run a pressure simulator model to test for breaches?"

"Permission denied," growled Hagues. "We'll be fine."

By this time several of the white coats and technicians were exchanging glances and looking nervous. The penetrating drone had risen to a piercing note that seemed to drill down into the very marrow of every living element on the research station.

At the top of the tower, Miguel felt the vibration, too, but his attention was grabbed by what he saw onscreen. The surrounding ocean was being whipped up, despite the fact that when he had come onto the tower, the night had been reasonably calm. In the wide space of ocean between the three towers, the storm was becoming even more violent. Waterspouts were erupting from the crashing waves and rearing high into the sky—sometimes for hundreds of feet— only to crash down again into the water. The ships and helicopters that had earlier been maneuvering to unload coal and supplies were beating a hasty retreat.

Then there was a crack so loud that Miguel thought all the windows in the tower would break, and he was sure he could smell ozone even inside the control room. Something like lightning that wasn't lightning streaked down out of the black clouds and exploded into the water, sending up a huge waterspout, higher than any twister that had yet risen. Blue electrical light illuminated everything for miles around. The whine had become a shriek that tore at Miguel's senses—consoles and machines seemed to join the ruckus in sympathy—and outside the window the waterspout took on a life of its own, stretching up into the sky, and opening a whirlpool-like chasm within itself, so that looking at it, you could not be sure whether you were looking at some mighty tornado or a black vacuum that disappeared deep into the sky.

Miguel could feel a deep existential fear, not only within himself, but emanating from every single person in that room downstairs. He was gazing at the most frightening apparition he had ever seen.

30.
COMPLETING SEA-NOMAD-BECOMING

In contrast to the bright ocean and daylight outside, the hut's interior seemed as dark as night. But once Jade's eyes adjusted, she registered the familiar surroundings, and saw Kreh-ursh's dim form lying on the ground in its curtained-off alcove. She walked forward, taking the jewel fish stone from the creamy pouch around her neck. Kneeling beside the boy from the sea, she displayed it on her palm.

Taashou moved slowly around Kreh-ursh and eased herself to the ground on his other side. She gazed long and hard at the jewel fish stone but did not try to pick it up. Jade was at a loss. In the last few days, since Kenzoh's tale, all her and Geh-meer's actions had been aimed at bringing them to this point. Yet now she was holding the jewel fish stone, and she had no idea what to do with it.

She heard muffled voices outside, and the door curtain of the hut was pushed aside. Geh-meer entered, followed by Kreh-ursh's parents. Taashou frowned but said nothing. They came and settled themselves around

Kreh-ursh's pallet, as well. Once there was stillness, Taashou leaned forward and gently lifted away the light covering that covered the boy's upper torso. Jade gasped. His back was a suppurating expanse of blackened and festering skin. Taashou gestured toward a spot in the center and looked at Jade. She needed no words or mind speech to tell Jade what she should do. Jade reached out and placed the pale pearl from the jewel fish lightly on a spot on Kreh-ursh's back. She withdrew her hand, and together they all waited.

Soon Jade became aware of a soft crooning noise. At first she thought that it was Kreh-ursh's mother humming, attempting to console herself about her son's condition. Then she realized that it was Taashou who was making the sound. Imperceptibly, the old lady's humming became stronger and more rhythmical until it was an incessant nasal whine that seemed to tear up and down Jade's spine. She wasn't sure how long she could remain in the same room as that unpleasant drone, but she gritted her teeth, determined not to do anything embarrassing like jumping up or crying out to silence the old woman, which she felt like doing. The sound just intensified.

Glancing back at the jewel fish stone, from which, in her annoyance, she had taken her eyes, she was shocked to see it flickering with a grayish light. Silvery gray reflections fluttered across Kreh-ursh's back. The stone itself appeared to be clouding with gray and darkish smudges.

Taashou's chant was strident now and pierced each person in the room until all five were threaded on its plaintive monotone, like fish hanging from a cord. She noticed little change in Kreh-ursh except for those lights, now of different colors, shimmering over his skin. She longed to scream out, to silence the shahiroh's chant, but she had lost all power of movement, of will. It was as if all the energy in her body had been appropriated by the force of that sound and bound into a single purpose.

Then, very gradually, she saw how the strands of light over Kreh-ursh's body were entwining like web-bing or mesh, enclosing and protecting him. Within that glow, the stone from the jewel fish had darkened. It reminded her no longer of a pearl, but of a sooty marble. She saw now that the light over Kreh-ursh's back was leaving silver trails like those a snail might leave on a leaf, and each shone with the glow of freshly healed skin.

Sitting on the rocks at the end of the bay, Jade reflected on the awe-inspiring process she had experienced a few hours earlier. The jewel fish stone rested on a rock close to the sparkling surf nearby. Though its interior remained dark and cloudy, the surface was gradually fading to its original sheen. Taashou had suggested she allow the stone to cleanse itself near water. So she had come out onto this rocky promontory, away from the village. Here, where a light breeze blew in from the sea, she could collect her thoughts and watch the stone return to neutral after the healing it had performed on Kreh-ursh. She felt a strong bond with it, as if she had become its guardian.

Gazing over to the beach, she saw that a small crowd had begun to congregate above the high-tide mark. Among them were shahiroh in their blue robes, Shahee in green, and other villagers in a mixture of browns, reds, and grays. Geh-meer stood with her family, her arm around her father, Rrehn-ursh. Her brothers, the twins, Teh-tur and Teh-bhoush, and little Chang-eh stood with them.

Kreh-ursh appeared from the village, walking with difficulty between his parents and supported heavily on his father's arm. Wearing a new tunic of a lighter shade of green than Geh-meer's, he moved slowly down onto the beach. Fresh bandages wrapped his otherwise bare arms and legs. His mother carried a woven basket. He walked along the beach to a last lonely pile of driftwood that waited out beyond six burnt circles in the sand, and sat down on a nearby canoe. Jade could tell that even that exertion cost him. His mother placed the basket in front of him, and from it he took two sticks and a package of wood shavings and moss.

After catching his breath, he stood up and walked alone toward the wood stack. There he knelt down carefully and began the arduous task of making fire. Several times he tried and failed. For a while it seemed as though he were too weak to go on, but he persisted. Finally, he managed to create a tiny nest of sparks and tip them gently into his prepared moss bed. A wisp of smoke arose. A flame caught. People cheered as the bonfire took off. He smiled around at everybody briefly, then slumped, at the end of his strength. His parents rushed up, along with others, to lift him away from the heat of the flames. They sat him gently on the beach above the high-tide mark, where he could watch his fire.

His eyes roved over the beach, and he saw Jade.

Come over.

People stared, for he had broadcast in a way that everybody could hear. But before she could get up, think about whether she should abandon the jewel fish stone, he had slumped further. Immediately, his father and another man picked him up and carried him back toward the village. Jade decided to remain where she was.

Turning her attention back to the sea and the jewel fish stone, she lost herself in the hypnotic wash of the ocean for a while, until a slight noise behind her made her look around. Geh-meer was perching on the rocks beside her. They smiled at each other.

You have saved him, and all of us, stranger.

Jade nodded. The jewel fish stone worked.

All that remains is to save my brother.

Geh-meer frowned and squinted at the horizon.

I have to get back to my world, Jade insisted. *I have to see if this works on Kyle ... my brother.*

Geh-meer glanced at her, but she did not look comfortable.

I understand how you feel. I have brothers whom I have looked after always. Our mother died giving birth to Chang-eh. Since then, I have been ... no replacement for her, but my father could not have raised us on his own, so I have done my share of mothering.

Jade nodded. She envied Geh-meer her strength and self-sufficiency. She felt similarly protective about Kyle.

However, Geh-meer continued. *We have found the way to defeat the death stain, and the rift is closed.*

Jade felt a sinking in her stomach. It couldn't be …

Taashou has called a council of the shahiroh, and we are to attend … when Kreh-ursh is well enough—

To open the rift?

To … decide on the best future course of action.

But I helped you!

Yes, but the council must consider what is best for all life in this ocean. Nobody knows whether the rift can even be commanded, or whether it would connect to your world again or some other. It has always appeared in our world in a random way. Besides, opening the rift may simply endanger this world needlessly. I'm sorry, Jah-eed, but I thought you should know that it is unlikely they will agree to help you.

Jade was stunned. So it had all been for nothing. She might never see Kyle or her family again.

So then why did that ghost … your friend … save me, and bring me and Kreh-ursh together…? It doesn't make sense! I must get back to my world!

Kaar-oh died…. Geh-meer seemed to choose her words carefully before going on. *The dead do not normally have so much power. I do not know what happened…. Somehow by leaving our world, he … changed, gained some sort of freedom from death…. I need to talk to Kreh-ursh to know what happened. But you should not think that he was necessarily trying to help you. He may have done what he did for his own selfish ends. Kaar-oh was never very predictable when he—.*

Now Jade was angry. She stood up and grabbed the

jewel fish stone, clasping it in her fist, not caring whether it was fully cleansed or not.

He was your friend! You should know whether he was good or not ... or don't you consider that in your friendships? Do you only ever consider what is convenient for yourselves?

She strode away up the beach. Tonight she did not care where she slept, but she wanted to be away from these selfish people.

31.
COERCION

At the top of the tower, Miguel stood staring at the phenomenon onscreen. On a whim, he went to the door and listened. He could hear nothing, so he turned off the lights, unlocked the door, and eased it open.

To his right was the landing with the iron staircase he'd come up, a set of elevator doors beside it, and in front some wide glass doors. Rain beat against their thick glass, outside of which he could see the helipad. The real spectacle occurred beyond. In the space between this tower and the other two, the storm had transformed itself into that screeching column of water and wind. Even through the soundproof glass he could hear it screaming and feel its very un-nature. As he studied it, his eyes were drawn down into nothingness, so that it seemed like he were gazing into a deep chasm, which was this rift that had appeared, tearing the sky asunder, and everything in this world would be swallowed within it. Yet if he could sail through, he might go home.

He checked himself. Home? Where was home? Home for him was to become Shahee, one of his tribe. Miguel realized that the thing was controlling him, the force that could cause him intense pain if he didn't do its bidding. It was easier to obey and save himself that pain than to try and remember where he should be going, whom he should save ... Jade.... He knew the name but couldn't place the person. Was this somebody from his world? He thought so. He knew she was a girl, his friend. He didn't know who the Shahee were, only that he had to go through the whirlpool to find them. They were home.

A noise behind him made him turn. Rena stood there, watching him. She was one of those who would deny him becoming Shahee.

"I suppose you thought you had me tricked, you runt."

It seemed pointless to affirm the obvious, so Miguel said nothing.

"Just you and me, runt. Screwie's had to carry the Head down to the infirmary."

Sorry about that, Miguel almost mumbled, vague as to what she meant, but realizing it had something to do with how this boy he inhabited had tricked the gang.

"You always seem to be the one to take the punishment, don't you?" she sneered, nodding at his cast. "Why do you think that is?"

Wracking his brains for any escape from this situation, Miguel just shook his head. But uppermost in his thoughts was the pain, that he could take no more pain. Jade's explosion. The laboratory.

"I had nothing to do with that explosion," he panted.

"So you've been telling us." She smiled. "But you and me, right here, right now, isn't about getting answers for my boss—it's just because I don't like you."

Miguel's heart sank. So pain was unlikely to be avoided. Yet his priority was getting back through the rift. She was in the way.

As Rena stepped toward him, he moved forward and stretched out his hand. Kaar-oh shouted with all his might, and a mind-punch of white noise hit Rena square in the forehead. Her eyes went glassy, and she sagged back into the wall behind her. Miguel moved past her and tapped the elevator call button. Turning, he watched the security guard slide to the floor as if she were drugged. The elevator doors opened, and he stepped in. Soon he was dropping toward the dock.

32.
KAA-MEER-GEH

The Great Canoe, paddles driving into the surf, surged toward the headlands. Alongside, Kreh-ursh raced along in Kreh-otchaw-oh, skipping in the Great Canoe's wake, dueling with the waves, while Jade traveled with Geh-meer in her craft, Shur-ursh-oh. Kreh-ursh was ecstatic to be back on the water. Tacking to and fro to either side of the Great Canoe, they sailed past the headlands and out to sea. Then they turned their canoes shoreward, but in a direction the three young people had never taken before. Following the Great Canoe, they closed in on the forbidding profile of Kaa-meer-geh and the hidden harbor at the red volcano's base.

The beach on which they landed consisted of gritty red sand, like ground-up bricks, thought Jade as she shouldered her rucksack and stepped ashore. She walked up the beach, then stopped, realizing she was the only one who had come ashore. Turning back, she saw Geh-meer and Kreh-ursh still sitting in their canoes, seemingly reluctant to set foot on the beach.

She looked across at the Great Canoe. Seeing that

none of the Shahee had landed, either, she felt as if she had inadvertently committed some taboo act. The Shahee had brought the Great Canoe gently in to nudge the beach so the half-dozen shahiroh might jump to land without wetting their feet. Then the sailors back-paddled, and the canoe withdrew out into the bay.

Glancing back at her friends, she saw with relief that Geh-meer was now standing on the sand, while Kreh-ursh was gently easing himself over the gunwale. Though his burns had all but disappeared, he still couldn't move without difficulty. She was amazed by his recovery. The jewel fish ritual had taken place just after midday on the day they returned from the sacred island; by early evening he was walking and had been strong enough to light his symbolic fire.

Jade and Geh-meer had made their peace less than an hour after Jade stormed off. The beach had begun to cool rapidly as dusk fell, and she grudgingly accepted hospitality with Geh-meer's family, grateful to sleep in a warm hut. Yesterday, though Jade had chaffed at the delay, she accepted Taashou's insistence, backed by Kreh-ursh's mother, that Kreh-ursh rest, so Geh-meer had shown Jade around the village while Kreh-ursh lay in his hut and slept.

It was incredible: Less than two days after being healed, Kreh-ursh was now strong enough to sail his own canoe, but as she watched him ease his way onto the sand, she realized that he was still pitifully weak. Striding down the beach, she waved Kreh-ursh away and took hold of Kreh-otchaw-oh herself. Quickly, she dragged the canoe up onto the soft sand above the tide mark. At that moment, Geh-meer was doing the same with her own craft. Straightening from the task, their eyes met, and they grinned. It was a little disconcerting to share such a feeling of complicity—Jade had never had many female friends. Yet she and Geh-meer seemed to be made in a similar mold, though they had been born entire dimensions apart and came from utterly different cultures.

The young shahiroh, Lehd, came down toward them.

Hoh-ee. Welcome to Kaa-meer-geh.

Hoh-ee, they all murmured. Jade found that she had picked up the greeting, though in mind speech, languages were irrelevant. So she wondered how she knew the word was hoh-ee and not hello, though the two words felt intrinsically different in her mind.

They followed Lehd up the beach. Kaa-meer-geh contained no vegetation. Everything was the same gritty, powdery red, so it wasn't clear where the line of the beach ended and the cliffs began. The gritty sand just seemed to curve into vertical escarpments, up which a narrow staircase had been cut into the rock. This was the path they took. It zigzagged back and forth across the cliff face, taking them gradually higher. Halfway up, Jade looked out over the lagoon and saw the Great Canoe, tiny now, just clearing the headlands on its progress back to Rrurd. It was a brown stick on the clear azure water, framed by the brick red of the volcano's slopes. Down below on the beach, she saw a handful of blue-gray specks —the shahiroh who had remained on the beach — clustered a short distance from where their canoes lay beached. Behind her, Kreh-ursh was huffing from the climb. She waited for him.

Lean on me. You are not fully recovered.

He just frowned at her and stepped past, continuing on his way. Jade felt hurt. Since the explosion, and on arriving in his world, they had been unable to speak. First, he had been unconscious, then surrounded by his family and the other villagers. Yet he was her reference point, the one person in this world she had known slightly longer than anyone else. He was the only person who knew her world, even if only slightly. She had hoped they might find a space to sit together and talk, but everything was moving so fast, too quickly for her to cope. Already it seemed that Geh-meer was becoming her friend and Kreh-ursh a distant stranger with whom she had shared a brief adventure long ago.

Finally, they reached the top of the cliff. Ahead was a wide plateau, stretching up to where a stream tumbled down a gorge from the volcano's heights. Nothing grew near the stream, as nothing grew anywhere on the island. To the right of the gorge, a rising progression of rock terraces evolved into another cliff, harboring several shadowy cave mouths. Blue-cloaked forms were coming and going from the caves.

Lehd nodded toward them, indicating that was where they were headed. No words were needed. They climbed from terrace to terrace, up a series of carved stairways, and by the time they reached the top, Kreh-ursh was wheezing. Jade watched Geh-meer go to him and roughly place his arm over her shoulder in a way that brooked no denial. It was what she herself should have done, she thought, and the thought annoyed her.

Entering one of the cave mouths, they walked down a long tunnel before coming out into a wide natural courtyard in the rock, open to the sky. Doorways dotted its circumference. Lehd pointed to one.

You can rest in there. You will find beds and fresh water and other minor comforts. We are calling a council of the shahiroh. You will be required, but probably not for a couple of hours, so rest if you need to, but be ready when I call.

He nodded to them each in turn, almost formally, and walked off into the labyrinth of tunnels under the volcano.

A third of a tide cycle later, Kreh-ursh came out of a cave into the wide space. Instantly he stopped, shocked to see the circle of stakes driven into the red earth before him, with a line of brooding huts beyond. A large number of shahiroh were gathered there, but against the sea of blue-gray, one moss green tunic stood out. Geh-meer was standing alone in the center of the space and had raised her hood against the flurries of red grit and dust that were whirling in small zephyrs around the space. This was the image from his vision; it was happening.

Heat rose to his face, and his heart began to thump. It seemed he could not find enough air to fill his lungs. Sagging against the cliff wall, resting his hands on his knees, he stared at the ground and tried to recover. So his visions were coming to pass. First there had been the finding of his tree on the sacred island of Zjhuud-geh, the tree that had become Kreh-otchaw-oh, his canoe; then he had seen the sea life and how it was killed by the death stain; they had fished the jewel fish; even though he had not been involved personally, he had been cured by its pearl; and now this—he was seeing the ceremony on Kaa-meer-geh unfold. The green-hooded figure he had seen in his vision was Geh-meer, not himself. She would soon take a wooden cup and drink, and then.... So the final scene in his visions would also come to pass: He had seen himself, scarce years older than he was now, traipsing through an arid desert—he had been parched and dying. He had seen himself fall and lie unmoving. So it was his fate in a few years to die, far from the sea or any water, with nobody to see him perish or mark his passing.

So be it. If that was what would come, then it must. He knew now he could devote himself to the saving of Shah, to the life code. This was why he had been saved; his sacrifice would achieve it. Then a few short years from now, he would cease to exist.

His breathing steadied, and he wiped his brow. From now on it was vital to make these few years count. Could anyone ask for more? Once he was sure he had recovered his composure, he pushed off the wall, and walked on. Now nothing could be wasted; every exper-ience must be treasured and squeezed of its fullest potential. He stepped out into the open space and walked across to greet Geh-meer.

33.
BRAVING THE FAULT

As the elevator doors slid open, a huge wave crashed onto the dock, setting it awash in a high swell. Water swirled even into the elevator, drenching Miguel. He held tight to the open doors as the wash surged back toward the ocean, pulling at his legs and threatening to drag him with it. There was no sign of the powerful launch by which Dr. Hagues had arrived. Miguel doubted that his own tiny outboard dinghy would have survived such an onslaught, either, assuming Hagues' employees had not taken it from where he'd left it tethered.

Here was the rift, the fault, the whirlpool passage—an open doorway leading back into his own world, and he was alive again! Once more he was living inside a human body, one he could control, instead of a sleeping child. He raised his hand to stroke his talisman, safe in its scarlet bag. The question was, could he still use his wave-crafting and windcalling skills? If so, he might surf the current back through the rift and into his own world.

He thought of his mother, Kehl-een, of how sad she

would have been at his death and how overjoyed she would be to see him return, albeit in another body. But she would soon get used to that. He was her baby. Since his father died when he was small, his mother had relied on him to be her helper, and he had been—until death had taken him from her. That was over now. He would go back and make sure she never wanted for a thing.

Another wave washed over the dock. Experimentally, he curled his mind around it, attempting to shape it to his will. He felt its brute power yield to his will. Satisfyingly, the wave curled and pulled itself higher, drawing back from the place where he stood so as not to drench him a second time.

Yet he found it difficult and was intensely aware of inhabiting this new mind, as if he were trying to paddle a canoe that was not quite built to his own proportions, as though the gunwales were too high, or the paddle too short for him to use comfortably. He was also aware that the original mind lurked somewhere below, though he did his best to keep it down. This was easier than it had been with the child. The younger one seemed to have some sort of inner resilience that had bucked against his control constantly, and despite its being sick and dying, he had felt that it had been using his energy as much as he, Kaar-oh, had been able to draw on its life force.

He reflected on the process that had brought him here. Would he still be able to see into the future once he was back in his own world? It had felt incredible, coming through the rift—like an awakening or a rebirth. At one moment he had been just a fuzzy presence attached to his talisman as if by gaark-teer hooks piercing his flesh, existing more in Kreh-ursh's mind than in the real world; then they had been drawn together through the rift as if through a rainbow.

Instantly, he had seen his entire life and Kreh-ursh's, future and past, laid out bare, yet not in a physical way. It was as if his consciousness had become a lamp penetrating the darkness in all directions. True, he could no longer see very far back in his past—only up to a year or so before his death. And the distant future was likewise dim. Yet lit up within the glow were the girl Jah-eed and her brother and also, enigmatically, the mythical creature the jewel fish. As if they were strands of kree-eh, he could follow the young people's lives and see how they entwined with Kreh-ursh's, with his own, for suddenly he had a life again. His energy burned bright. He saw how he might inhabit a human body afresh, found that point at which he might connect with the boy Kai-al, but knew that to do so he would have to pull the girl into contact with Kreh-ursh and somehow make her aware of the jewel fish, though he could not see how she might use it. She was needed to save Kreh-ursh, and he did not want his friend to die. One day they would again sail together across the great ocean of Shah—if only he could get back to his own world.

However, several hours after taking possession of the child Kai-al, he had noticed his prescience begin to wane, as if his lamp were growing dimmer. What would happen if the child died? Would he be extinguished with it? Immediately, he had focused all his strength on helping Kreh-ursh and Jah-eed, for if they saved the child, he might secure his own existence.

He became more firmly entrapped within the unconscious child's body, and even as the child faded, it was increasingly more difficult to control its life force. Then a miracle occurred: the boy Mee-ghel found Kaar-oh's talisman. The boy had barely settled that scarlet pouch upon his breast when Kaar-oh felt himself pulled back toward it. It required him to make a sickeningly scary leap across the dark abyss of nonexistence, but it had been an easy decision to make. He could see that the child Kai-al would be dead within a few hours, so his choice to embrace life was obvious.

Kaar-oh looked out at the raging sea and the pillar of water and fear that towered above him. Could he wield his skills sufficiently through this alien mind to make the journey? If only he had completed sea-nomad-becoming, he might know that he had mastery over the Shahee's skills! He felt fear of the rift at the foundation of his being. That was normal, though, wasn't it? And anyway, he had virtually completed sea-nomad-becoming by ac-companying Kreh-ursh; it was almost the same.

Taking a deep breath, he stepped out of the elevator cubicle and onto the sea-washed dock. Instantly, the full violence of the storm beat against him. With the sea surging across the surface of the dock, he could barely stay on his feet. Another big wave would be sure to wash him off. It was now or never. Turning his face toward mu-orl-rehn-baa, he raised his voice and began to chant.

34.
FEAR OF OPENING

J ade closed the journal, and let it lie there on her lap. She had by no means come to the end of the close scrawled handwriting, but what she had read aston-ished her. It explained so much about the research station's purpose and why Dr. Hagues had chosen to site it offshore from Mauri Cove.

But she also knew that she had to stop what he was doing. Hagues was prepared to sacrifice this beautiful ocean for his dreams of power. She would get back there and stop him—for the sake of her world, and for Kreh-ursh's world. Now she also knew that she could. The rift, or the fault, as he called it, could be opened, directed, if you had the coordinates—and an awful lot of energy. But you needed to know where you were going before you could plot your route. She must convince the shahiroh to try and open the rift. It was the only way she could save this world or her brother.

She stood up, picked up her rucksack, and headed out toward the dusty central space where Lehd had told them they should gather. She could hear a light humming from somewhere, maybe inside her own mind, as if she sensed a headache coming on. She didn't feel concerned, though; rather, she felt confident and assured.

As she came out into the sunlight, she saw Kreh-ursh and Geh-meer ahead of her. They were standing in the center of a wide circle of wooden posts planted in the ground. Before each post stood one of the shahiroh. The sight of that ring of blue robes against the red earth caused Jade to hang back against the rock wall, wanting to watch what would happen. However, Lehd saw her and waved her over. He pointed to where her two friends stood alone in the center of the circle.

As she walked out into the center, he joined her, walking alongside as he explained:

We want the three of you to open your minds to the combined council of the shahiroh. The shahiroh will see and share everything you have experienced in your journeys to and from the other world....

Everything? Jade felt uncomfortable. *What sort of things do they see?*

Another shahiroh stepped out of the circle. He was short and muscular, approaching middle age, yet with an air of authority that Jade had so far noted only in Taashou.

This is Bhawl-dresh-oh, Lehd introduced. *He will lead the process.*

The council will see and feel all you have felt. Bhawl-dresh-oh seemed to have read her fears. *Yes, they will experience every emotion just as you did, what you felt in every situation.... But they are discreet. We will only look at the last two days and not pry....*

I don't know— Jade didn't feel like having a gaggle of old people peering into her mind and knowing every emotion she had experienced over the last forty-eight hours. An alarming thought occurred to her.

And will Kreh-ursh and Geh-meer...?

Bhawl-dresh-oh nodded. *This is not a private process.*

Jade stopped, looking at her friends, who stood waiting for her a dozen yards away. If this was the only way.... She glanced at Lehd, then back at Bhawl-dresh-oh. *Only if you can assure me that through this process we can reopen the rift.*

Bhawl-dresh-oh would not meet her eyes. *We need to pool the knowledge you have experienced....*

So Geh-meer had been right. The shahiroh did not plan to reopen the whirlpool and send her back to her world.

No. She shook her head. I will participate only to help my brother.

Bhawl-dresh-oh stared at her. *We do not need you. It is enough with Krehursh and Geh-meer....*

In that instant, Jade realized with a shock that these people's objectives were truly different from her own. Geh-meer's words on the beach came back to her. Looking around, she was impressed by the assembled shahiroh facing them from the circle. She, Kreh-ursh, and Geh-meer were the only ones there not clothed in blue: She was in brown and her friends in their Shahee green.

The shahiroh, en masse, appeared a potent force. A patina of magic seemed to shine from their robes like a heat mirage in the dusty space. She felt intimidated but also enraged. How was it that after she had come through so much—destroying the factory, braving the rift, finding the Lake of Stone, fishing the jewel fish and curing Kreh-ursh—they would refuse to help her by reopening the rift? She realized that all the gathered shahiroh were listening. It was time to seize her moment. She addressed the circle, broadcasting as loudly as she could.

You know my need, why I searched for the jewel fish ...

Child—

The old woman Taashou was suddenly at her shoulder, though Jade had not noticed her approach, nor even seen her since they had arrived on the island. It was almost as if the shahiroh had appeared out of thin air.

We indeed know your plight, the old woman said. *I have seen your brother with my sight. He is important to us and will be more important to saving our world than most of us here can know. I have tried to make this clear to those assembled—*

Then why won't you help me?! She screamed, in a mental roar she doubted she could ever equal with her own voice.

The majority must decide, admitted Taashou. *And they have done so.*

We need to see. It was Bhawl-dresh-oh who spoke. *And ... feel the references, the physical places that you have experienced, in order to know how to link to them. It is vital we collect this knowledge to be able to protect our world in the future.*

But not now? You won't open it now, for me? She

thought of Kyle. He would die now if she couldn't return. She wondered whether she might bargain.

I won't do it. I won't share the knowledge I have unless you swear to me that you will open the rift to take me home.

She was aware of Kreh-ursh and Geh-meer standing a few yards away, watching her argue with their elders. She found it difficult to meet their eyes, unsure what rules she might be violating with her defiance. But if this were truly the only way she could get back to her world and return to Kyle, she must try. Even so, she didn't trust these detached and impersonal elders and hated that they would be able to read her every last thought and feeling.

As if to confirm her thought, Bhawl-dresh-oh shrugged. *As I said, we do not need your mind. With—*

With mine and Geh-meer's, you have enough?

At Kreh-ursh's mind voice, Jade looked over to see him and Geh-meer standing shoulder to shoulder. Now Geh-meer spoke up.

Kreh-ursh and I have conferred. We will do this only if we help Jah-eed. Taashou, you know—

Shahee, Lehd snapped, *you will not defy the shahiroh again!*

Then a silence fell, or else the discussion in mind speech was blocked from Jade's hearing. She looked around. Even if Taashou stood with them, they were four against the combined majority of all the sea callers. If the process worked, and they got through, would the stone even work to save her brother the same way it had worked for Kreh-ursh? What if it was only successful on people from this world? Jade looked back at

Taashou to find the old woman scrutinizing her intently. But it was Bhawl-dresh-oh who spoke:

We cannot do it. It's against the life code. The importance of one life cannot be put before that of every living thing.

Jade felt as if her world were spinning around her, dragging her down into the deep. Once again she was underground in the tunnel behind the cave and thousands of tons of rock were pressing down on her, crushing the breath from her lungs. Dimly she was aware of Kreh-ursh and Geh-meer on either side, supporting her, but at the heart of her vision, deep in the whirlpool's vortex, she could see only Taashou's shrewd dark eyes, observing her. And at the center of her mind was a single stark realization: Her bluff had failed; the people of this world would not help her. She was stranded here—forever.

35.
GOING HOME

From some place deep inside himself Miguel realized it had been a mistake to follow the path of least resistance and give in to the oppressive presence that had now taken hold of his life, for he could now find no mental foothold to force himself upward again into the clean air. Instead, he was trapped deep in a sightless place that he felt he had visited only in his darkest and most sinister nightmares. Restlessly, he writhed, searching for a path up into the light, but the force that had hold of him pressed down, controlling every breath he took. Miguel felt as if he were suffocating, and knew he would die if he didn't find a way out to where he might breathe once more.

Kaar-oh stood on the very edge of the dock, washed by the waves that crashed about him. Using his mind, he had raised the water into an intricate dance about himself. The surf now lashed and snaked around him like a miniature version of the mu-orl-rehn-baa that dominated the sea and sky ahead. Yet he failed to find the required point of resolution to choose a wave and throw himself in, to surf home through the rift. His fear, naturally, was real—like every human being, he felt it. Could he defeat such fear again? He had braved the rift once and triumphed—even though he had been carried unwillingly through, attached to his talisman. But he could do it again, he was sure.

He thought of Geh-meer. Would she be pleased to see him? Would she accept him in this new form? She might even find this boy's appearance more attractive than his own. He was set to dive, but something still held him back, and he cursed himself for whatever it was, the factor that made him doubt.

Behind him, the elevator doors opened, and he turned, allowing the waves to subside into a more natural pattern. The scientist, Dr. Hagues, stood there, and his relentless gaze barreled into Kaar-oh—though Hagues could not know who he was. Still, Kaar-oh felt unnerved.

"Boy!—Miguel—that is what you call yourself, isn't it?" the man shouted over the gale.

Kaar-oh nodded. So did Hagues, as if in sympathy.

"I can tell you where the girl is!" Hagues peered at Miguel. His thinning hair was plastered to his scalp, making him look, with his large glasses, like Edvard Munch's portrait *The Scream*. "She went into that storm!" His arm shot out toward it like a harpoon.

Kaar-oh glanced around at the rift. *What girl?* he thought. *The one I saved so she could help Kreh-ursh? The same one that Mee-ghel seeks? So she too is Twilight Crosser—now why is he telling me this?*

Hagues looked at him, as if he were sizing him up. "You don't have to be scared of that storm," he grated.

"It leads through into a magical world."

Kaar-oh said nothing, and simply waited.

"You may not believe me," Hagues' voice came even hoarser over the sound of the wind. "... but it is a beautiful world … of tropical islands, blue seas, lovely ladies … Do you understand me, boy?"

Kaar-oh didn't, but he nodded anyway. But what was it that the old man wanted? As an experiment, he released his pressure on the youth Mee-ghel slightly and felt his prey inhale mentally, breathe in that tiny chink of consciousness Kaar-oh was allowing him. The old man continued talking, and Mee-ghel sucked gratefully at the words.

"If you go through there, and do as I ask, I can offer you a reward as rich as any you have ever dreamed of."

All Kaar-oh dreamed of was surfing through the rift—no need for this man to pay him. Yet he wanted to hear what the man had to say. "What's that?" he called.

"Whatever you ask." Through the driving wind and rain, Hagues' smile was like a gnashing of teeth. "Tell me what you want."

Then a memory arose, one of those belonging to the creature he inhabited. He saw the kree-eh, channeled through some sort of transparent reeds. They had kree-eh here, in this tower! That was the presence Kaar-oh had felt when he first came on board! The old man wanted to harvest the kree-eh. But the kree-eh was sacred, everybody knew that. It could only be harvested under the strictest conditions a couple of times a year, and only for a very special purpose. He stared at the man, wondering what he could want with such a life form.

"You see, I can't go through there … but you could be my partner, my right-hand man on that side of the fault." The man winked, but then seeing the puzzlement on Miguel's face, he continued on another track. "Sorry about our little misunderstanding earlier. I didn't mean for those goons to hurt you. Allow me to make it up to you … Tell me what you want! Do you need a boat? I can get you one."

A boat would be better, easier to cross—or would it? The basic need—his need—must be so great that his desire would overcome his fear. But he felt the fear deep inside himself, stronger than before, and knew he could not do it. Not yet anyway. Not unless he could make this boy whose body and mind he was using travel across the rift. Then Kaar-oh might return in the same way he had come—dragged across the void as an involuntary passenger. He could force the boy Mee-ghel to cross, apply so much pain that he would do anything to escape it.

"You cross the fault, make those people do business with me," Hagues urged. "And when you come back, I'll make you a partner in this company. You'll be one of the richest men on the planet. How would you like that, bo—eh, Miguel?"

Kaar-oh jabbed a shaft of pain down into Mee-ghel's brain and felt him writhe. He smiled and released the pressure slightly. Kaar-oh smiled at Dr. Hagues. The man's eyes appeared like pale blue minnows wiggling through the goldfish bowls of his glasses. Kaar-oh needed nothing the old man had to offer though, since, despite his fear, he could force the creature he controlled to navigate the rift. He would simply be carried home on its back.

"What can you offer me?" he challenged. "I need nothing that you have."

It was as if the old man then locked onto his consciousness in the same way that Kaar-oh had jumped aboard the mind of this Mee-ghel. It was amazing how powerful he was, despite having no mind speech or other mental powers. The man smiled more broadly.

"Come closer, so that we may talk."

Kaar-oh knew he himself was too powerful now to be tricked, so he walked across to the elevator, keeping the wash of the waves at bay with his wavecrafting skills. He found he was able to control this boy's mind more effectively with every passing moment. He stopped a couple of yards away from Hagues, surprised to note he was taller than the old man.

"Hoh-ee," Dr. Hagues murmured. Kaar-oh was shocked. Hagues chuckled. "Yes, I perceive you now. I didn't before, thought I was dealing with a simple local boy. But with everything you have done," Hagues' hand indicated the waves shaped around Kaar-oh like a protective cowl, "You have shown yourself to me as one of the Shahee."

Now the boy Miguel-who-was-Kaar-oh was unsettled. "I am going back to my home," he said. "I need nothing from you now the rift is open."

Hagues studied the boy. "Everybody needs something. When I look at you, I see a youngster from this world, yet one who can control water like the Shahee. Exactly who or what you are, I can't say, nor do I know how the two worlds have become mixed in you. But I sense there is something you require very badly."

Miguel-Kaar-oh shrugged. To be accepted as Shahee? This man could not give him that.

Hagues' eyes sparkled and he smiled more deeply. "You need power, and that is something I can offer."

Hagues somehow knew he had ensnared his prey, and he continued to talk, to weave ideas and visions before the boy's eyes. Gradually drawing out responses, he learned who he was and how Kaar-oh came to be standing there on the dock of Hagues' tower. Hagues wove that information into his offer, and painted an imaginary future that appeared irresistible.

So when the boy Miguel-who-was-Kaar-oh finally turned toward the mu-orl-rehn-baa, it was with a fresh resolve. He strode to the edge of the dock again. Summoning a huge wave that was sweeping toward him, he wrapped it tightly around himself and dove into the sea. A silver bullet-shaped wave soon surfaced and began to power through the ocean toward the whirlpool passage.

36.
OBLIVION

J ade lay on the ground. Her eyes were closed, but she felt the grit in her hair and against her palms where they lay in the dirt, and knew it as the volcano's dirt, the dust of her prison. She was still on Kaa-meer-geh, in this world where she would spend the rest of her days. Sensing a figure kneeling beside her, close but not touch-ing, she knew it was Kreh-ursh. A hubbub of sound, mental and spoken, was arising around her, as if some great catastrophe had been unleashed, and when she could resist no more, she opened her eyes to see his worried face.

What happened?

You fainted, but—

What? What has—?

The rift has opened.

All she could focus on was the color of his eyes, a soft shade of hazel. Then she realized what he had said.

They opened it? How?

He shrugged. She didn't dare breathe, but a moment later she sat up. She felt hot and sticky. The sandy arena was a cauldron under the relentless sun.

So I must go through.

He frowned, but she ignored him and glanced around. Shahiroh were hurrying in many directions, though mainly toward Kaa-meer-geh's beach. She sensed mind speech humming through the air as the blue-cloaked figures communicated urgently with each other. One of them saw that she was sitting up and came over. It was Taashou.

You have been given your chance, girl of the deep green. Do not waste it.

She met Taashou's gaze and, after a moment, nodded. Then she glanced at Kreh-ursh. It was clear what was in both their minds: This was the moment when they must begin to say goodbye. Though they had barely met.

I am going home to save my brother. She spoke clearly in her mind, trying to betray little emotion, yet distress seemed to dribble from her thoughts even as she formed them.

I am coming with you.

We may not get back. Who knows if the rift will hold? This is your world.

Children! Taashou hissed, unconcerned at any embarrassment they might have that she had overheard their conversation. *Decide now, or the rift may close. It is still most of a day's journey away.*

Kreh-ursh reached down and pulled Jade to her feet. As one, they began running for the beach.

How else would you get there anyway, he panted, *when you have no canoe?*

He had a point, Jade admitted, as they ran.

Kreh-otchaw-oh lay beached where they had left her. Together they dragged the canoe down to the water. Before launching her, Kreh-ursh stepped back. Kneeling, he scooped up a handful of Kaa-meer-geh's gritty substance—maybe the last touch he would feel of his land, a world from which he had already been torn. Like Jah-eed, he had become no more than a fluttering scrap of rag, afloat on the universe, with nothing to connect him here, or anywhere—except maybe this dust. With his free hand, he eased open the leather pouch containing his talisman, and poured some of the red dust inside so that it surrounded and protected his personal totem. Might it serve him as a beacon to remind him where he had come from—or draw him back, should he stray too far from these seas.

They launched the canoe and paddled out into the bay, Kreh-ursh behind in the steering position, Jade in the bow. The sun beat down from a pale sky, and the harbor's red arms around them let not even a hint of breeze stir the water, so its surface appeared as flat as burnished steel. Leaving this world afresh, he knew this time it meant more than simply conquering his fear and departing for an unknown adventure: He might never again know a place he could call home, for wherever he landed, he would remain an alien.

Kaa-meer-geh: another part of his vision fulfilled ... the shahiroh's secret island. He, Geh-meer, and Jah-eed had been to the place where only the wise ones go. He had done what he had been asked to, and saved his world, the ocean of Shah. No reason remained for him to be risking his life afresh—not for the sake of his people. He was doing it for this alien with her need to save her brother. And yet the life code …

In the middle of the bay, Jah-eed turned and looked back. Her eyes—so often stony, unwilling to show any vulnerability—now seemed soft, almost smiling, even if her face remained set. She looked fearful, as was natural, since they were heading for the rift.

To return through mu-orl-rehn-baa, experiencing that feeling of losing everything, everyone he knew once again, was terrifying. And he was now Shahee…. Did he have to do it, sacrifice himself for this girl?

Before they had left Kaa-meer-geh, while Jah-eed was lying on the ground in a faint, Taashou had spoken to him.

How do you feel? Her black eyes scrutinized him.

Kreh-ursh was not frightened of her anymore. They were equals now. She could no longer look as deeply into his soul as she had that time adrift on the ocean in a storm, before he had become the twilight crosser. Now he knew how to protect his mind. He nodded slowly. *Ready … I know where I am going.*

But many things might still happen before death.

Wind howled, and the sea raised waves into shuddering peaks that came crashing down into their own deep valleys. The canoe was being tossed like a piece of bark through the maelstrom. Jade clung on for dear life. Kreh-ursh's chant raged against the storm, his voice hoarse and strident. She could feel his presence simply as a vibration of power, as his chant transformed the molecules of his world into twisting patterns of wind and wave. The canoe trembled with the force of his magic.

She was wracked with remorse: They had left the volcano island in such a rush, it was low on the horizon before she realized she hadn't said goodbye to Geh-meer, who had been such a friend to her. But it was too late to go back—they were approaching the whirlpool.

She trembled with what she saw ahead. The rift rose up, still some distance off, but she was scared to go through the dark tunnel a second time. Yet she had no choice. Kyle lay dying on the other side.

Light had fled from the day. Clouds mustered and swirled, sucked toward the rift. The jewel fish marble felt warm against her sternum, seeming almost to hum, sucking in the power it sensed from Kreh-ursh, from mu-orl-rehn-baa, and from the universe they were about to leave.

She didn't belong here—she knew that—but dread sat heavy in her bones. How could Kreh-ursh be so brave? She wished she was strong enough to face this test again, but she realized now that she wasn't. Her brother would be the sacrifice. She loved him, but she couldn't face the raw terror of being stripped from her dimension once more. She turned to look back at Kreh-ursh. Then she gasped.

Kreh-ursh, look!

He turned. In the near distance, a small canoe bob-bed. It was just near enough for them to make out that the blue form crouching in the rear was Lehd. Yet Jade was pointing at a spot about halfway between them and the canoe. Gilded with flashing phosphorescence in the rift-induced twilight, a bullet-shaped mass of surf was speeding their way.

"Geh-meer!" they both shouted.

In moments, she had reached their canoe and was heaving herself aboard—an eerie repetition of how she had rescued them on the far side of the rift. She smiled as she sat dripping onto the floor of the canoe.

Geh-meer, but why...?

I am a twilight crosser, too. We are in this fight together.

Kreh-ursh met her gaze, then glanced at Jade and smiled. But she noticed that his eyes were troubled, even as deep down inside of her a chord was sounded. *If only.* She was glad Geh-meer was here, as she did not feel strong enough to go through with this final effort. And she knew they could not consider anything else until the threat of the rift had been overcome.

Terror began to gnaw at them all as the whirlpool snagged them in its grip. Already they were rising up the horrendous slope.

Look!

Ahead, another figure was surfing through the water, but this one was being spat from the whirlpool's gullet.

"Miguel!" Jade screamed.

"Kaar-oh!" Kreh-ursh and Geh-meer shrieked.

But they were now rushing steeply up the hideous slope, approaching the maw. Jade screamed again, but they were all screaming, both mentally and aloud, along with Kaar-oh's piercing laughter. But Geh-meer was standing, both terror and rage twisting her features.

No, Geh-meer! Kreh-ursh roared. *Be strong!*

I am! A sacrifice is needed. I will do this!

Geh-meer!

But she had already dived into the water and was struggling and thrashing with the swimmer, pulling him upward again. The frenzy of their clashing water magic seemed like an explosion in the void of the tunnel. The canoe and its occupants were for a few seconds drawn along in the same rush as the flailing swimmers. Then those two seemed to veer aside and disappear into the blackness of the tunnel wall. A sharp sort of crack! sounded, and then Jade and Kreh-ursh were crouching in the canoe alone, plummeting into the depths of the rift.

Kreh-ursh, save her!

He stood, roaring power, desperately trying to pull back, but Kreh-otchaw-oh was trapped now in the rushing tunnel, and they plunged down the sides of the whirlpool. They were both screaming, eyes wide with their own fear as the horror overwhelmed them. Jade and Kreh-ursh and their craft were swallowed, and vanished into the rift between dimensions.

HERE ENDS

LAKE OF STONE

TURN THE PAGE TO READ THE
FIRST CHAPTER OF

BEHIND THE WORLDS

BOOK IV
OF
SEEKING THE JEWEL FISH

I.
THE LOST ONES

Like a blur of tumbling chorn-weed, a posse of taagaag-ee—five beasts and their riders—flowed over the rippling plain. Though the sun stood high, leaching color from the sky and scorching the hardy grass, the travelers seemed impervious. The heat was unremarkable for the season, and they were used to journeys such as this. They rode at a regular, unhurried canter—having made good progress since dawn, and aiming to go much farther before dusk — knowing it was the best pace to cover ground.

Raa-gehd-ur, one of the two leading Taagaag-ee, was furious. The two days' ride to reach the sea, plus a third tossed in a flimsy outrigger at risk of his life, had been for nothing. Meeting the sea witch and her kind had told him little and solved less. Then, with empty hands to show for their pains, the two brothers were jostled back into a canoe with a bunch of seasick city dwellers. Perhaps the only minor consolation was that neither he nor Doh-ayd-dur had been so stricken. Even after they had made landfall, though, and swung up into the saddle with their waiting comrades, camp had lain two days' ride away. So six days lost from the Roh-saahn season, when every able hand was needed for rounding up the yearlings. To say he was angry was understating matters.

"Raa-gehd, what's that?" His right-hand rider and younger brother was pointing beyond his taag's horn at a sort of dimple in the sky above the western horizon.

Raa-gehd didn't answer immediately, but as they rode, he studied it. Gradually, the cloud darkened and swelled until it had become a swirling mass. Something about it rang familiar, but he could not recall where he had seen such a thing.

"Looks like a mighty beast of a storm is on its way," was all he ventured.

His thoughts continued to churn to the rumble of the taagaag's hooves. Their trip had not been totally in vain, but he would think hard before answering such a summons from Taashou again. He did have news: They had met the Lost One, Daakohn-bhah-ehl-bhah-her, had seen him with their own eyes, and even talked to him. It wasn't exactly that he hadn't believed in the existence of his father's long-vanished brother, but the man was talked about almost like a fairy tale. Around the camp fire, they still told stories of this Taagaag-ee who had forsaken his tribe and crossed through the twilight. This uncle of his had apparently broken in a creature huger and more horrendous than ... Bhaanj-kraag-oer. He smiled. The myth of the fire-snake was his favorite, about that evil dragon from the primordial dawn that was slain by the mother of all taagaag, impaled upon her horn to save their human forebears. Daakohn-bhah-ehl-bhah-her had apparently tamed a beast so large it could live neither on land nor in the air but must swim through the ocean like a sea skur. But he and his brother had seen it for themselves—not to mention smelled its fetid stench—proving its existence, and his uncle's.

The dark clouds were drawing together across the entire sky, and the air felt stretched—as if the world about them needed to shriek. Something was wrong.

"Can you feel it?" he called to his brother.

Doh-ayd nodded. "The taagaag are nervous, have been since early this morning. Something's about… Is an earthquake coming, do you think?"

He didn't know whether it was the brewing storm or something else that was upsetting the creatures, but he was doubly keen to reach camp and consult with their father. It wasn't just about having seen their father's brother: He was worried now about how best to protect the herd. A big storm might prove disastrous with all the unbroken yearlings corralled together. The very same thing had happened once when they were boys, and they would never forget it: a herd of several hundred head of taagaag stampeding through the camp. Three among the Taagaag-ee had died. One of those had been Hurm-eh, their baby sister.

He pondered how to approach his father when they got to camp. Their last meeting had been as near a fight as the two had come in the time since his father had ceased riding out with the herd. Raa-gehd-ur was now the head Taagaag-ee, effectively the tribe's leader, but his father's name, Daak-gehd-meer, still held more sway over the people than Raa-gehd-ur could command. To his eldest son's mind, Daak-gehd was a bit too fond of showing this in public, never allowing his son to assert his own authority.

Shaan-shel, his taag, shied at a hidden burrow, reclaiming Raa-gehd-ur's attention. He could sense all five of the creatures cantering around him becoming increasingly skittish. This was dangerous: The taagaag could be ridden when they were calm, but when these creatures became possessed by the taag-skeel-ert—a sort of passion or panic that bore them away—they were capable only of fighting or mating, and it was safest to set them free. Shaan-shel's jitters meant she was becoming more difficult to control.

"We'll need to dismount soon, Doh-ayd," he called, and glanced over his shoulder. The other three riders, a short way behind them, were also having difficulty with their taagaag.

"Let's hold off as long as we can," suggested Doh-ayd. "If we follow a path north, we may be able to give the storm a wide enough berth to keep them manageable."

It was risky. Any rider trying to remain astride a taag when it gave in to taag-skeel-ert risked disembowel-ment on its horn. The taagaag lost any memory of domestication for the time they remained possessed. But gazing now at the wild coil of cloud before them, Raa-gehd recalled the sea nomads talking about the ocean-borne tornado they were calling the rift. It would not do to get caught in something like that either.

Reining Shaan-shel in, he studied the rising storm.

Could this somehow be related? Was that what was affecting her? His taag ducked her head, brandishing her horn menacingly at the clouds. A wind was rising. He felt her fear and terror of whatever was forming on the horizon.

"Does that not seem like the same problem they have out on Shah?" he asked the other riders as they came up.

"So far inland?" Raa-gehd's father's oldest friend, Ben-faad-lehr, shook his head. "It couldn't happen here, I wouldn't think." He paused. "Could it?"

Raa-gehd shrugged. Ben-faad had not traveled out to the floating town with them, claiming he was too old for such adventures. So what could he know of that alien danger except the words Raa-gehd and Doh-ayd had repeated, which had come from the mouth of the sea witch? The winds around them were becoming stronger, whipping at their clothes with a violence unnatural to the season. Soon grasses and small clods of earth were being torn up and flung in random directions.

"Okay, we ride farther to the north," Raa-gehd decided. "As far and as fast as our taagaag will take us. With luck we can work around this thing without having to dismount."

He raised the hood of his cape, wishing he could protect Shaan-shel as easily. Grit and dirt flew at the taagaag and Taagaag-ee as they struggled on, stinging the hides and eyes of both creatures and riders.

Beyond the gray turbulence that now lay to their left, Raa-gehd-ur saw a wavering column rising through the sky, dark with the airborne loam of the prairies. The very sight of it caused his heart to stop, and he had to force himself onward despite his foreboding. Besides the fear, he felt another emotion arising: desperation. Through this whirling false dusk, he now sensed the column's geographic location. While he still couldn't tell its size or relative distance, he realized it was approaching from the exact direction of the camp.

Coaxing the taagaag northward was more difficult than expected. However hard the riders urged on their mounts, and despite their fear of the storm, the vortex of cloud continued to pull, as if drawing them toward its center. Raa-gehd urged Shaan-shel faster.

But the riders felt the unease of their creatures growing. The animals were noting some vacuum of mental energy. With dread Raa-gehd probed and found that Shaan-shel could hear no answering sentience from the direction of the camp, no flicker of life from among her fellow taagaag. Even from so far away, he thought she should have heard distant murmurings from her herd mates. But she encountered only silence. Maybe they were still too far off.

Flying debris now meant that neither taagaag nor riders dared open their eyes more than a tiny slit to peer ahead. Their pace had dropped from an easy canter to a dogged walk, but by moments the roaring column came on.

"Doh-ayd, we must dismount!" With that he threw himself off Shaan-shel's back, expecting her to be borne away by taag-skeel-ert and gallop off. But surprisingly, she kept her head lowered, and just stood trembling in all her limbs. Taking hold of her bridle, he pulled her northward. She allowed herself to be led. His brother and the other riders were doing the same.

In staggering steps they advanced. The day was now dark. Wind struck at them, laden with dirt, stones, and uprooted plants. Raa-gehd wrapped his arms around Shaan-shel's head to protect her from the debris and pulled her along like that. She remained docile in terror, head lowered, her horn pointed horizontally north-ward. Over her neck, Raa-gehd saw the vortex whirling relentlessly closer until it was towering above, radiating terror into man and beast alike. Sensing the nearness of death, he tried to prepare. Then a rock hit his temple, and he fell into the dark.

PURCHASE

BEHIND THE WORLDS

AT

WWW.POBLESECBOOKS.COM

K. EASTKOTT

Born on a South Pacific island, from his first foray into *The Hobbit* at ten years old, through writers such as Ursula K. Le Guin and Anne McCaffrey, K. Eastkott spent his formative years submerged in fantasy and science fiction. At nineteen he set out to discover the world and spent the next twenty-odd years living in and moving between countries such as Spain, Australia, New Zealand and England. He writes contemporary fiction as Kevin Booth.

You can get loads of free stuff and stay updated with K. Eastkott and Poble Sec Books by signing up to our mailing list at:
www.poblesecbooks.com
Facebook: www.facebook.com/poblesecbooks
Twitter: @PobleSecBooks

www.ingramcontent.com/pod-product-compliance
Lightning Source LLC
Chambersburg PA
CBHW050318110726
47899CB00007B/2293